HORNS AND HAIR
OF THE
HIGH COUNTRY

Horns and Hair
of the
High Country

Lloyd Antypowich

Rev. date: 10/23/2013

To order additional copies of this book, contact:
Xlibris LLC
1-888-795-4274
www.Xlibris.com
Orders@Xlibris.com
140927

CONTENTS

Look for other books published by Lloyd Antypowich

A Hunting We Did Go

Lloyd is an avid hunter. He loves the mountains and has great knowledge of animals in the wilderness. This book makes the reader feel like he is along on the journey with him, experiencing the beauty of nature, the thrill of the hunt, as well as the acceptance of being outwitted by the animal he was stalking. Time and again, people have said, "I felt like I was right there with you."

Moccasins to Cowboy Boots

This is the journey of the author's life as he followed his dream to become a rancher. Filled with history and humor, his journey takes him from the homestead where he was born in the northern wilderness of Saskatchewan to Northern Alberta, where his family logged and owned a sawmill. Later he worked in the oil fields and road construction then became a farmer at Stettler, Alberta, and a miner at Elkford, British Columbia. But his dream carried him into the South Cariboo, where he bought a ranch at Horsefly, British Columbia, and became a logger to help support his dream. This is not a diary of his life; it is a humorous and determined journey of a man who refused to accept the concept of being unable to achieve any goal.

Louisianna Man

This is a fictional book inspired by a man the author spent an afternoon with while he was in his late teens. This man had lived a remarkable life and was happy to share his harrowing life stories as well as showing off the spots in his back where buckshot still lay under the skin. The hero of this story, Tom Menzer, is the author's reincarnation of this sort of a man. Tom Menzer leaves his home in Louisiana to follow his dream. This is a story in the best of historical Western tradition, filled with drama, insight into the Indian culture in the late 1800s, the role of the white man as they pushed them aside, the struggles of a man who had a foot in both camps, and his journey into Canada to avoid the conflict. It is a tale well worth your read!

Chip Off the Old Block

This is a tribute to the author's daughter, Cherie Jackson. They have a very deep bond and are very much alike, except she is a female who comes in a very tiny package and he is a big, strong male. He is constantly amazed by what she accomplishes and is delighted that she shares his love for the mountains and loves to be out in them with her companion, who is a guide and outfitter. A wonderful read about a courageous, little package of dynamite—a true chip off the old block.

DEDICATION

To all the people who have been hunters and gatherers—even if there aren't that many of you left—and to all those who still love to hunt the backcountry, I share with you some of my years of enjoying hunting in the mountains and my knowledge about the animals of horns and hair in the high country.

Sections of this book are purely fictional, written from my interpretation of the animal's point of view and based on my understanding of wildlife as gained through years of learning about them in their natural habitat. Others are true incidents that have happened in my lifetime while encountering animals in the wild or when hunting.

ACKNOWLEDGMENTS

To all the people whom I have shared my bannock and campfires with and who have been company to me on my trips into the mountains. May there always be a wilderness for you to go to.

To my wife, who is not a hunter but is more knowledgeable with the computer than I am and who dealt with the publishing procedures with Xlibris for me. You are very much appreciated.

To Doug Jones, who did the editing for this book and gave me encouragement to make this into a book.

INTRODUCTION

The Rocky Mountains, a mountain range, runs down from Alaska through Canada—separating Alberta from British Columbia—and south into the United States of America. People work and play in it; they even sing about it. There are volumes of memoirs written about its development that go back to when it may not have been the pleasant place it is today.

In its infancy, when it was first being developed when from a way down within itself, eruptions of gas and tremendous heat caused rock to melt and, in its liquid form, came bubbling up to the surface and formed what we know today as the Rocky Mountains. The volcanoes and ashes must have been horrendous—it formed lakes and valleys, and today, we look at it in awe of its entire splendor. The magic of time has made it into one of the world's most sought-out places. And people from all over the world come to look at it and take pictures to ski, to climb, to hunt, to fish, and to just experience the feeling of being in one of Mother Nature's most wonderful creations.

I had the most wonderful experience of seeing it one night while I was flying from Kamloops, British Columbia, to Calgary, Alberta. The pilot came on the intercom and welcomed everyone on board. He said it was one of the most beautiful nights to be flying, and if anyone would like to come to the cockpit, he would show us what beauty really was. I loved to fly, so I raised my hand quickly, and the stewardess led me to the cockpit.

When I entered the cockpit, the pilot introduced his copilot and himself, and I introduced myself. He looked at me and said, "You must be a cowboy."

I said he was close, because I was a rancher. He asked me if I lived in Calgary. I said no; actually, I was from Horsefly. He said he knew where that was, but he wondered what brought me out to fly with them that night. I told him that I was going to a directors' meeting for the Canadian Limousin Association. He said he knew someone who had something to do with Limousin. He was associated with Ward Air at one time. I asked if that would be Jack. He turned and looked at me and asked where I said I came from.

I said, "Horsefly."

He said, "You sure fooled me."

It is simply amazing where you can make friends; there I was, thirty thousand feet above the Rockies, talking to someone whom I had never met before, and we knew the same people. He asked if it wasn't just the most beautiful night to be flying. And it truly was.

The snow that covered the mountains had a special glow in the moonlight. The stars were so bright, and there didn't seem to be a cloud in the sky.

The pilot pointed out a light that was flashing off to our right, about two o'clock, and said, "That is our sister ship going back to Kamloops."

He flicked a switch on the control panel and got a reply immediately.

That was the most wonderful flight that I've had in my entire life. I love the mountains, and at the time, I just had a look at them from thirty thousand feet in the moonlight. The towns of Banff, Jasper, and Lake Louise and the hot pools of Radium and Miette are truly a place for people to enjoy and relax themselves, not to forget all the other ski resorts where people come to bask in the beauty and ruggedness of those majestic mountains.

Within its magnitude, the Rockies hold many important resources: water, forestry, mining, tourism, ranching, and a wilderness that is home to many birds and animals. Because of its rugged wilderness, there are still many places that man has very rarely visited. It has been home to many world-record sheep, elk, deer, moose, goat, grizzly, black bear, and cougar. And not to forget our feathered friends, like the majestic bald eagle that soars over the mountains and valleys looking for its next meal. When the Creator looks down on his handiwork, he must be really pleased, for it is truly beautiful.

But man has made plans that have dramatically affected all the wildlife that lived in the region of the Rocky Mountains, but no one ever consulted the wildlife to get their opinion of what effect it would have on them.

Tourism has demanded more access into the wilderness. That meant more roads, lodges, and services; and to pay for all this, the powers that be said, "We will sell a license to hunt birds and animals, and to those who are nonresidents, we will charge an even bigger fee. On top of that, a killing fee would be imposed should they be successful."

The railroad was the first to come into the mountains, then the roads came, and they went in all directions. They eventually made it all the way through the mountains. The roads all led to the railway as all the products were moved for long distances by train. Train was the fastest means of travel at the time. It created work for the people to service the rail lines and to man the water and coal stations, and people soon settled in areas that looked good to them, and they delivered products to the train, and the train delivered supplies back to them.

Then the telegraph line came, and it took more men to build and service that. And then there was need for more coal. That meant more mines. There would be sawmills that would cut lumber for all the new houses and bridges that were needed to service all the new development, and soon the Rockies were developed. There would be trails for hiking and riding, and people came from all over the world just to see this wonderful wilderness. And so the plan was passed.

The people were happy, but the wildlife took a heavy hit and have been trying to adjust to it ever since. And to add insult to injury, the oil companies were granted a right to do seismic work in the exploration for oil and gas, and if they were successful, they would be granted permission to drill for oil. The mining companies wanted their kick at the can as coal was discovered all through the Rockies and new mines opened up. There were little towns built to service the hot springs and ski hills, and the Rockies became a haven for tourism.

The development was supplied by the demand; the people from the prairies wanted to go to see the ocean, the warm climate, the fruit trees, and such. The train could deliver supplies that came to the ports of Vancouver to the prairies. And the Rockies were no longer the wilderness that it once was.

There were rules and regulations made to better help regulate harvesting of the wildlife. And in some cases it worked, but in others it did not. But once again, the biggest losers were the birds and animals. Some people want more eagles, others want more wolves or grizzly bears, and so goes the balance of nature, like the pendulum on a clock swinging back and forth. One wonders what it will be like a hundred years from now. Let's hope better heads will prevail and all will work for the better.

In the chain of command, Mother Nature's law has been that every species that is a predator will prey on each other, depending on size and numbers, in order to survive. Prey animals are animals that have the greatest sense of vision when they are looking straight ahead and have an eye set in the front of their head, including man.

All other critters have their eyes on the side of their head and have the greater vision of any object on the side of it. Some have eyes near the top of their head—which allows them to see better the movement of objects above them—like the gopher and marmot. But they all have peripheral vision; they are known as flee animals. The horse, elk, deer, sheep, goat, and antelope can and will run at the first sign of danger.

Hunger is what drives the prey animal to become dangerous to all other critters, and although they depend on other species to survive, they will become much more aggressive when they are faced with starvation.

Each species has a built-in mechanism that works to their advantage. The horse and antelope have very good eyesight and can run real fast and can flee from danger. The moose, on the other hand, has a very good sense of smell and hearing and can flee from danger before it gets too close to it. The porcupine does not rely on sight, smell, or flight but is equipped with a covering of very sharp quills that will stick into any predator that tries to harm it. The skunk, on the other hand, has a defense mechanism, which is to spray a very offensive-smelling liquid that will turn a lot of predators off. The rabbit and ptarmigan change color to change with the seasons to make them less noticeable. The wolf, cat, and coyote have an eye set that comes from the front of their head, and eyes that can focus very intently on its prey and can sneak up on it. Along with that, they usually have a good sense of smell.

Man has a brain that makes us superior to all other animals and, from the sense of all other animals, makes us the most feared of all. The eagle has such keen eyesight that he can spot a mouse from a mile away. The turkey buzzard has a good eyesight, but he excels so much better on sense of smell. He can smell carrion ten miles away, when he is circling and riding the thermal air currents. He—along with the crow, raven, eagle, and other small birds—is the garbage collector of the wilds.

The eagle will and can kill mice, marmots, gophers, young goats, and sheep. But he is known for his ability to fish, and is very good at it. He is a bit of an opportunist and will take advantage of anything that comes his way when it comes to food.

One day, in mid-April, I had a mare that was going to foal, so I put her in an enclosure where I could watch her from the house. The snow had all been melted for a number of days, and the grass was a good inch tall, so I decided to let her foal out in the small enclosure instead of putting her in the maternity pen in the barn.

In the morning, I was up early, and to my surprise, we had two inches of snow on the ground and a new foal as well. I hurried out to see if there was something that I should do for the mare and foal, but that little foal was bucking around and looking like she enjoyed playing in the snow.

What caught my eye was an eagle that had her claws hooked in the afterbirth and didn't want to give it up. It had one claw hooked into it and was trying drag it away. It had dragged it about a hundred feet in the snow and was just sitting there. It was not really of any danger to the mare or foal, so I just left it there. I put the mare and foal in the barn, and after making sure the foal had sucked, I was going up to the house to have my morning coffee when I noticed that the eagle had nearly devoured all that afterbirth and was just sitting on the ground. I thought it a bit unusual that it would just sit there, so when I got into the house, I got the binoculars and took a good look at her. And she was still there. She looked a bit overloaded, so I had my coffee and toast, and got my camera to take a picture of the new foal. When I left the house, the eagle was still there, so I went into the fence to see if there was anything wrong with it. I got so close to her that I could take a few pictures of her. She was just overloaded and couldn't fly.

When I came back from the barn, I went to see if she could fly, but she could only make it up to the top rail on the fence. That was one overloaded eagle. When she tried to fly again, she made it to the limb that was lower down on a poplar tree that was outside of the pasture where the mare and foal were in. The next time I looked, she was gone. I guess being that her breakfast was a little bit more slippery, it may have gone down a little easier and that may have caused the overload. But I will bet that when she regurgitated that load for her chicks, she had enough to feed them for a week.

One day, my wife and I were fishing on Quesnel Lake. The weather was perfect. The fish were hungry and biting good. We were in about a hundred feet of water and two hundred feet from shore. I had a seven-pound lake trout on and had him five feet from the boat. While I was getting the net in position to net this fish, an eagle swooped down and picked him up and was going to leave without saying good-bye or thank-you. I jerked on the line, and the eagle tore a piece out of that fish two inches deep and six inches long.

Taking a look at that fish, I said to my wife, "That is one for the birds."

I bopped the fish on the head and threw it into the water. Before I had the boat back to trolling mode again, the eagle had that fish and was flying to shore, where he kind of crash landed. The load was too heavy to get enough elevation to go to where they had their nest. So when I say that eagles are opportunists, it means they will take advantage of any kind of a situation when it comes to food.

The grizzly, on the other hand, has a good sense of smell and can see and hear fairly well. He is very unpredictable; what he does one time he may not do the next. Because of his size and strength, he really does not always give way to other animals. And there is one thing that you can almost always rely on: if he has a kill that he has covered, he will guard that with his life. Many a hunter has been killed or severely mauled because they have unexpectedly walked onto a bear kill.

Bears are very fast for short distances and will give you very little warning. They can be very cantankerous if and when you are trespassing in their territory, but they will usually let you know, and it is highly advisable to get out of there as quickly and quietly as you can. A grizzly is best approached out in the open using the wind to your advantage. One only has to see a grizzly trying to catch a marmot on a mountainside to appreciate their strength. He can dig out rocks as big as a five-gallon bucket and throw them around like popcorn. Bears can also decapitate a cow with one mighty swing of his paw with those six-to-seven-inch claws.

Men and wolves are his only enemies. Wolves will put the run on a grizzly if there are enough of them. But two or three won't do it. There are grizzlies killed with one arrow, and then there are grizzlies that have been shot with magnum rifles and still kept coming, only to kill or severely injure the hunter. They can be very hard to stop once they get that adrenalin going.

Yet I personally know an Indian lady who shot a seven-foot grizzly with a .22 when she was hunting rats in the spring of the year, and killed it with one shot. His hide hung in the bar of the Slave Lake Hotel for many years. But if you plan to go hunting grizzlies, I do not suggest you use a .22.

You will do just fine if you don't make any sudden surprises or get between her and her cubs. The other time they do not like being disturbed is in the breeding season. Should you come upon a pair in that state of love affair, you could find yourself fighting to save your life.

The elk are somewhat of a herd animal. The bulls gather a harem of cows for the breeding season and fight to keep as big a heard as they can. They fight ferociously with other bulls to show their supremacy. After the rut is over, they are quite beat up and look for a quiet place to recuperate and heal their wounds. They become friends with their previous rivals and share the same meadow while they heal their old battle scars. But they are usually not too far away from the herd of cows and younger bulls.

SECTION 1

Ronnie, the Royal Elk

It was a nice spring day; the sun was shining on the mountainside. There was only the odd cloud in the sky. The grass was growing everywhere it could find enough good soil to send its roots deep enough to get moisture and nutrients that would sustain its growth. The new leaves were out most everywhere. The wood violets and Indian paintbrushes were blooming along with the Saskatoon and huckleberry bushes. The smell of all the new foliage was so pleasant and the air so fresh; it was a perfect place to give birth to a new elk calf.

The mother elk had frequented this place several times before and was convinced that she had picked the best place to give birth to her calf. Somehow she felt this calf was going to be a special one. His daddy was a majestic one; he had six points on one side and seven on the other.

He controlled his herd with such authority, and his bugle was so majestic and authoritative. He was ferocious when defending his herd and never let another bull elk enter his space. His ladies seemed to respect him, but he was always so alert to any danger, the herd felt safe under his control. And now she was prepared to give the genes that run through her baby a chance to prove themselves.

As she lay down to relieve the pain that was starting to tell her the birth was very near, she hoped for a fast birth as this was a very vulnerable time for her. There were predators that thrived on killing the young elk calves or her as well, predators like the grizzly and black bears. She must not take too long to get this job done. She bore down as hard as she could, and yes, things were starting to happen. She could feel movement. She bore down again and again, and she felt the fetus go through the birth canal. She lay there for a minute to rest, then she felt movement again.

Yes, it was here. She jumped up, and yes, there was a gangly little elk calf. She quickly started licking it all over and kept nudging it with her nose, and soon, the little guy was trying to get up. He failed on the first few attempts, but that was okay. It was Mother Nature's way of getting all the fluids out of the airways, because each time he fell on his side, it helped to expel a little more of the mucus. But soon he was upon his feet, trying to balance himself; then he took his first step and almost fell over. She continued to lick him until he was clean of all of the mucus.

By this time, he was looking for something to eat, so she encouraged him to where her milk was starting to drip from her teats. As he fumbled around, he got the taste of her milk that was now almost spraying on his little head. Then it happened! He found it, and did that ever taste good. He went from one teat to the other, and when he had nearly drained them, he felt so full he just wanted to lie down.

But they would go away from that spot where he had been born after she had cleaned up all the afterbirth. Then she would find a new place for him to lie down. The reason for that is to leave as little scent as possible where the new calf would lay in hiding until he got stronger and could follow his mother back up the mountain to the herd again.

She took him from that spot and fed him again then proceeded to go to the edge of a small meadow. There she found a nice shady spot for him by some small bushes, but first, she checked him over again. He'd had a bowel movement, and it ran down one hind leg, so she cleaned that up and nuzzled him so he lay down with his head flat on the ground.

Then she walked off into the meadow to feed on some fresh new grass that was full of nutrients that would make her milk real good to feed her new baby. She would keep a close eye on him as she filled her stomach. When she was full, she walked to a little creek that trickled through the meadow and had a good drink, then found a comfortable place to lie down where she could see her baby. The newborn calf has literally no scent to it; that is why she lay that far away from him so she could distract any predator that might come along. She checked him later that night and fed him, then she put him to bed for the night. In the morning, she went to him at first light, got him up, and fed him.

He felt frisky and wanted to frolic around. He enjoyed testing those long legs, and when he got them going all in the same direction, he could really motor. He had another long stringy bowel movement, so she took him to another hiding place. Once the colostrum had a chance to work through him, he would be having more normal bowel movements, and he would not be that easy to smell by other predators. The colostrum gives the newborn calf the antibodies that he needs to fight off any infection or unfriendly bacteria.

He enjoyed the little romp through the meadow and at times wanted to run ahead of his mother, but she kept him in check. When they got almost to the end of the meadow, she fed him again and then put him into hiding. It was important that he got to rest a lot because he was growing so much, and soon he would be romping around with all the other new elk calves when they returned to the herd.

While she was grazing, she noticed a coyote that was hunting mice in the meadow. He was getting too close to her baby, so she walked over in that direction, and when she was close enough, she charged at him. She did not get him, but her thundering hooves came so close to him that he left the meadow.

When he was in the shelter of the trees, he stopped to look back at her and wondered what had gotten into her. She had damn near killed him. He had gotten a lot closer to elk before, and they never acted that way.

They spent a few more days in the meadow. The mother elk would take her son for long runs around the meadow. He loved that he could run just as fast as his mother; his legs were strong and steady, and he could jump and buck without ever falling down. She decided it was time to take him back to the herd. There would be a few calves on the south slopes where the herd would gather to feed on the new grass and tender bushes.

The journey back to the herd took them up on some high mountains. Ronnie had never been this high before, but he enjoyed it. As they were going along, his mother stopped and gave a snort. She had gotten a scent of a grizzly bear. She made a detour and took Ronnie even higher, and his little legs were starting to get tired. She would stop only for a short while and then go again.

To Ronnie, this was not fun anymore. He was getting hungry, but each time they stopped and he would try to suckle, his mom would walk off, and they were going higher and higher. He had never been treated that way before. When they reached a place where his mother could see way back down the mountain, she stopped to let him nurse.

Then they were off again. This time, they made it right up to the alpine, and Ronnie thought that he was on top of the world. But he was so tired he just lay down to rest his little legs.

The grizzly gave up the chase and went on to look for mice and marmots. When Ronnie's mother was reasonably sure that there was nothing following them anymore, she lay down beside him, and they took a long rest.

The morning dawned to a beautiful sunrise, but it was cold and windy, and Ronnie did not like it. They had not go very far when they came to this big white thing, and it was even colder, but it was kind of fun to jump in it. This was the first time he had seen snow. They were so high up on that mountain that nothing was growing up there yet, but they had escaped the first attempt on Ronnie's life, and although there would be more, with each passing day, he would be getting stronger and stronger.

They worked their way down the mountain and came to a beautiful basin where the grass was lush and green. There was snow near the top, and that would feed the lower part of the basin with water and keep the grass nice and green.

As they got closer, Ronnie stopped. He had seen something move on that part of the mountain, and because he had never seen elk before, he was not too sure just what they were. His mother stepped back a couple of steps and licked him, assuring him that all was okay. There were lots of those things there; most of them were smaller than his mom, but one was much bigger. He was the one that came to greet them first.

Ronnie was hiding on the other side of his mom. When the big elk came to the other side to check Ronnie out, Ronnie would run around to the other side to hide. He played this little game of hide-and-seek until his mother reached down and licked him and kind of nuzzled him as much as to say "It's okay. Meet your father." Any of the other elk were not allowed to come within ten feet of Ronnie, or his mom would put the run on them. They would have to wait a little longer before they could be playmates.

Then one day, a new addition came to the herd, and Ronnie thought she looked so cute; she was so tiny, and she had all those little white spots on her back. He thought that he should be able to go and play with her, but her mom said, "Not so fast. There will be time for that in a few more days."

As each day passed, the sun got warmer, and it felt good to lie in the sun on the mountainside, and nearly every day, there were more new arrivals to the herd and on some days as much as two or three. But none were as cute as the first one with the little white spots. By now, they were allowed to play with each other, and she could jump and do all those fancy little moves, and he would try to mimic her, but somehow, his moves never turned out like when she did them.

Then one night, there was a lot of commotion in the herd there were snorts and stomping, and Ronnie knew that meant danger. In the morning, there was a mother who could not find her baby. She kept calling and running around, but she could not find it; a grizzly had gotten it. Then they saw the killer coming back, looking for another meal.

They all started to run for higher ground, but from the side of the meadow, another grizzly came out and had the advantage as he cut in front of them, and he was so close to Ronnie that Ronnie could smell the stench of the bear. He might not have escaped, but his mom put herself between Ronnie and the bear. She tried so hard to make it past him, but with one mighty swipe, it was clear his intention was to break her back. She was just a little too fast, and his long claw cut a slice down her hip.

They all ran as fast as they could, but the bear managed to catch one more calf. They ran up that mountain, and when they stopped to rest, they realized that another calf had been killed. Their old place was such a good place, but they could not go back to it, and they would have to find somewhere else to stay. When they had moved for about five miles, they found a nice place where the southern slope of the mountain had good grass and water. It was bigger, and they stayed farther away from the bush, so that give them a much better chance to see a predator coming. Ronnie's mom had a sore hip for most of the summer, and she kind of limped when she walked. Eventually it healed up and only had a scar to show where the wound was. Ronnie had learned so much in the short while he lived, and if it was not for his mother, he may not have been alive.

His father left, and Ronnie did not know where he went, but one day, his father showed up and had these funny things sticking out of his head; they were huge. He would keep rubbing them on the small pine trees until they were all shiny.

Then one day, he made that god-awful noise that scared Ronnie so bad that he came running back to his mom. His dad would round up all the cows, and any that did not want to obey would get raked over with his big horns. They soon learned that, and when he just tilted his horns, they would go anywhere he wanted them to go.

The other thing that he did was chase all the bulls out of the herd. Then one day, there was a challenge for the herd. They kept making that awful noise until the challenger came out into the meadow. They pushed each other all over the meadow, and finally, Ronnie's dad gored him in the shoulder, and it made a bad wound. Then he chased him right out of the meadow. But that was not to be the last time that he would be challenged; it happened over and over.

When the rut was on, he was not nice to be around. He would even chase Ronnie from his mom. One poke of those big horns told Ronnie that it was better to stay away than to get poked. This lasted for a little over a month, and then when the rut was over, things quieted down, but his dad had been beaten up quite badly. He walked with a limp and had many places were the hair on his body was all gone.

He pretty much stayed by himself and lay around. Winter was about to come to all the high country, and as the snow came, the elk would keep moving down the mountain to feed in the meadows. When the snow got deep, it was hard to get enough to eat some days, and they would browse on the tips of willows. The Chinook winds are a godsend to the elk. They can bear off a southwest mountainside and provide enough feed, even if some of it is willow tips. The bad thing about the Chinooks is that it will eventually freeze, and then the wolves can walk on top of the snow, and the elk are then at a great disadvantage and, in some years, suffer heavy losses.

Then there are the avalanches that can kill a lot in one slide. Ronnie was schooled by his mother, and she had been around long enough to have had firsthand experience. She would school him as much as she could in his first year; after that, he would be on his own because she would have another young elk to school and feed.

One night, it got real cold, minus thirty degrees. The elk had to paw all night just to keep enough feed in their stomach to keep warm. Then Ronnie heard a new sound, and it seemed to really worry his mom. It was wolves, and there were a lot of them. She made her decision real quick, and that was to leave the valley and head up into the mountain as far as they could go and hope that the wolves would stay in the valley.

The feed would likely be harder to find up on the mountain than in the valley, but she knew what wolves were all about. Her own mother had been killed by wolves, and she had watched as they ripped and tore at the elk herd that they were in, and it was a terrible way to die.

She was prepared to starve before she would let them kill her or her baby. So she led the way up, and it was very hard going. Some elk started to follow but then turned back. So now it was just her and Ronnie. They rested quite often as the way was steep and the snow was deep. They got to a place where the wind had blown most of the snow off the ridge, and there was feed but nothing for shelter.

They were both hungry, so immediately they started to feed on the grass that the wind had blown the snow off of that part of the mountain. Then they heard the wolves howl again and knew they were near the herd in the meadow. She found a little bit of shelter and lay down. Ronnie lay as close as he could to her. Then she heard the wolves again, and they were in the herd and would be having a real heyday.

She remembered what it was like. There were elk lying all over. Some were still alive but were hamstrung and could do nothing but lie there to be killed later. Ronnie's mom and he were both shaking, but it was not from being cold—it was from fear of the wolves.

In the morning, they got up and ate some snow as they were both thirsty. They looked for some grass to eat, but there was not too much, so they pawed and ate whatever they could find. It was difficult to get across a short little gully because the wind had blown it full of snow, and Ronnie's mom was leery to cross it for fear she would get stuck in it.

So Ronnie tried, and it was packed so hard he could walk right across it. But she was a lot bigger than him and was afraid to try. Ronnie started to eat on some grass, and she watched him. Finally she decided to try it and was able to cross over without any problem. They walked along that ridge and grazed on the grass that was there, but there was not that much as most of it had been eaten during the summer by the many elk that grazed those areas.

Then they came to a spot where they could look back down into the meadow, and they could see elk that had been killed by the wolves, and there were many. There were wolves eating on some of the elk, but lots were just lying around in the meadow. They would stay there until they had eaten most of the elk that they had killed, then they would go looking for some of the ones that were crippled but had gotten away because they would be easy to pull down.

There were lots of ravens and eagles there too. As Ronnie watched, he wondered if his little friend had been one of the unfortunate ones; she was so cute, and he hoped that someday they would be able to play together again.

The winter seemed so long, and the fat reserves that they had stored up in the summer where all used up, but there were a lot of others that looked real thin too. Then one day, this big elk came to the small herd that they were wintering with. He was thin too but was still so big. But his horns were gone. He came and checked every one by smelling them. Then he walked to where he had come into the meadow and looked back at the thin little herd and seemed to be saying, "Follow me," and that is just what they did.

They walked through the big timber and crossed a small river that was still open and running real fast. They all had a good drink, and it sure was better than having to eat all that snow. On the other side of the river, there was a big flat area that was kind of swampy; it had a lot of willow but also a lot of grass, and they did not have to paw too deep into the snow to get a belly full. They stayed there until the snow was starting to melt, and the sun was starting to warm the air.

Then one night, the wolves howled again; they were a long ways from them but it sure made everyone excited and they wondered if the wolves would find them. The next day, they all huddled close together, and the big elk led them out of the swampy area and across another fast little river.

This one was harder to cross because there was ice on the shore and that made it real slippery, but the big elk led the way and crossed it. Then Ronnie's mom and he crossed next, and that was enough to make the others do the same. They worked their way up the first bench of the mountain. The snow was nearly all melted off the southern side slopes and they had lots to eat. That was a good place because the sun was warm, and each day, the snow was melting.

Then a real strange thing happened in Ronnie's life. His mother no longer wanted him to come close to her, so she would bunt him, and sometimes it really hurt. She had never done that before, and he was really dejected. But then he noticed that some of the other moms were doing the same thing. He could not understand this strange behavior.

Then one day, the big elk tried to make friends with him and several other young male elk. He took them away from the herd, and Ronnie kept waiting for his mom to follow, but she just looked at him. The big elk found a spot where other animals had dug in the ground, and he started to lick the ground too. Ronnie smelt it and didn't think it was anything good to eat, but something made him try it. The big elk just kept on licking it, and soon all the others were doing the same thing. Then he led them to a nice cool spring where the water came out of the ground. Ronnie was real thirsty and drank long and hard, and so did the others. They were lying on the side of a nice hill side when the big elk got up and looked over the edge, and there came six elk. He went to meet them, smelled them, and then came back to the rest of the boys. It was then that Ronnie recognized his little friend. She was thin, but when he smelled her, he knew it was her.

Then there was another strange thing that happened to Ronnie. He was developing two itchy spots on his head, and he would rub them, and one day, he noticed that he was growing horns, just like his dad, but his dad had a lot bigger start than him. The thought came to him that if he was going to grow horns, he would like to kill as many wolves as he could.

His little friend's mother was one of the ones that the wolves had killed. That is why she was so thin, and it is a wonder that she even survived. But they were over with the winter, and from here on out, it should be easier to survive. And Ronnie would do everything that he could to make sure that happened. Ronnie's dad left them one day and didn't come back, but Ronnie felt that he could look after the little herd; after all, he had his little friend with him. He would take her to the mineral lick, and that would help her to get stronger. The ridge that they were on was big and just up above them was a bigger area still, so they were in a very good spot. The leaves were out, and all the bushes were blooming; the grass was growing good.

Ronnie had a set of horns that had two points and were fifteen inches tall. He soon learned that he had to be patient with them because they were still soft. One day, he saw a bunch of elk coming, and some had young calves with them. He was so excited he went running to meet them, and yes, his mom was there.

She had a new baby, and now, he was beginning to understand all the things that had happened to him lately. He was now an elk that was master of his own destiny. His mother was nice to him, but she was protective of her new calf. He was growing up fast and could understand that.

His dad showed up with that bunch of females but then left again. He was sporting a set of horns that Ronnie was envious of. Ronnie went back to his little friend, and if elk could talk, they had a long talk. Their long winter hair was nearly all shed off, and the green grass was making them look shiny. The herd was getting bigger and bigger; with all the little calves, there must be fifty or more. There were three young bulls with three points and one with four points and some spikes too.

The summer was good. There was lots of rain, and the pastures grew lush and green. Ronnie, along with several other young females, did a lot of exploring. They walked over mountain tops and enjoyed the cool breeze that they got in those hot July and August days. But soon the weather would change, and snow would come to the very high peaks.

Ronnie could feel a change coming, so he led his little herd farther down the mountain. His horns were getting itchy, so he would rub them on the small trees and bushes. His ivory points just shone, and he was so proud of them. He worked his way back to the herd only to find that there were a lot of elk there. And there was a lot of fighting and bugling going on, and his dad was right in the middle of it all.

As he approached the herd, a young bull challenged him for his little herd, and he was not to give his friend up to no one. Ronnie was an early calf and had grown very well for his age, and he could put the run on any of the younger ones. Ronnie looked at his father, and he saw a bull was giving his father a good fight. Then another bull charged him from the side, and they put the run on his dad, but he turned around so quickly and gored that bull real good and hurt him quite badly. He threw back his horns and made a bugle that Ronnie had never heard before, and then he was challenged by two bulls.

Ronnie didn't think this was fair, so he ran up and gored the bull right in the ribs. His ivory points were sharp and caused the other bull to back out of the fight with his father, but he turned on Ronnie, and Ronnie was almost up ended by the more mature bull. That was when Ronnie's dad charged the bigger bull and really put the hurt on him. Ronnie was very surprised as he had really never done that before. Then the second bull got Ronnie's broad side and just threw him over and was going to gore him again. That was when Ronnie's father got the elk right in the front shoulder and all most threw him over. It wrecked the elk's shoulder, and then Ronnie's father gored him from behind and chased him right over the hill.

He came back and bugled again. There were other lesser bulls that bugled, but when Ronnie's father charged at them, they would run, and soon, he had all the older bulls chased off that side of the mountain. When he came back to the herd, he looked ferocious; his eyes were red, and he was ready to kill anyone who challenged him.

He was puffing like Ronnie had never seen him puff before. As he approached Ronnie, Ronnie backed off, and Ronnie's father just stood there and looked at Ronnie. He seemed to be telling Ronnie, "Thank you for the help, but this is my herd. And don't you forget that."

Ronnie wanted to try and make that bugle sound, but his ribs were hurting, and he was not quite sure how. So he walked to the end of the ridge and tried. But it didn't come out like anything his father made. So he tried it several more times, and it became better each time.

Then there was an answer, and a lesser bull who was not a lot bigger than Ronnie came to challenge him. This lesser bull had been chased off yesterday, but this bugle did not come from the big bull that so severely beat him yesterday. As he came closer, he was very cautious, and then he saw it was only the little bull and was confident that he could run him off.

As they stood only yards apart, Ronnie made the loudest and meanest bugle he had ever made before, but the bigger elk knew he could beat up on Ronnie. So he challenged him, and as soon as Ronnie came head to head with him, he knew he was overpowered. He tried so hard to push the bigger elk back, but he just did not have the weight he needed. Then he made a very quick move to the side and slipped past the bigger elk's horns. Ronnie drove him in the shoulder as hard as he could and spun him around. He then took advantage of the position. He had the bigger elk in and gored him in the flank and hindquarter and did not stop until he had him run back off the ridge. Ronnie stopped, threw back his horns, and made another bugle as loud and fierce as he could.

The bigger elk knew better than to stick around when he saw Ronnie's father come running. Then Ronnie turned to walk back up the ridge and saw his dad standing there on top. If elk could give verbal expressions, Ronnie's father would have said, "Well done, son." Then away back on the ridge came a bugle, and Ronnie's father went charging back to defend his herd.

By the time the rut was over, he was hurting so bad that all he wanted to do was go find a nice spot where there was lots of feed and water and just lie around and recuperate.

Ronnie stayed with the herd. He himself was banged up some but felt that his place was with the herd. There were a few more young bulls that planned to stay and winter with them, mainly for their safety. They felt that numbers gave them greater safety. Ronnie, on the other hand, wanted to protect his friend and his mother from the winter and deep snow that was about to be coming soon.

What he did not yet know was the danger of man. He did not yet know that they could hurt you from a long ways away. He did not yet know the smell of them or the big bang they made, but he was about to learn soon.

The fall was real nice and warm, and the herds were in excellent shape to start the winter. Then one day, when they were traveling to a new feeding area, they got the scent of something. Ronnie did not know what it was, so he followed his mother.

Normally she would have run to the high country, but she stayed in the timber. They were still in part of the meadow that had a scattering of pine in it. Ronnie and another young bull were out in front running side by side. Right behind him was his mother with her calf right on her tail, and behind that was his friend. He heard the bang and saw the bull beside him fall. He was going to stop to see what he could do to help, but his mom ran right into him and kept him going. Then there were a few more bangs, but they did not stop to see what had happened. When they had run for a few hundred yards, Ronnie's mom stopped to listen. She got what she wanted, and then they ran for a long time. They could no longer smell or hear any danger, but as they checked the herd, there were three missing.

Ronnie was lucky once more; had his mom not bumped into him, he may have been shot. He was really confused, but then he had got a whiff of the scent of man; he would never forget that, but he still did not know what they looked like. In the short while that he lived, there had been three attempts on his life, but it all was such a learning experience and he would be all the better for it.

He relied on his senses and all that his mother had taught him, things like, "Never stop when they are shooting at you."

The winter was mild, and the elk wintered well. That was good for Ronnie's dad. He was really banged up and took a long time to get healed up. The wolves did their usual damage but to some of the other herds and not the herd that Ronnie wintered with.

But that seemed to be the cycle of life. The wolves, coyotes, bears, eagles, and ravens all fought the same cycle of life to survive.

When spring was in the air, the elk started their migration to the high country to feed on the new grass that grew on the south slopes. The cows would go into seclusion during the time they gave birth to their newborn calves and then bring them back to the herd to learn the ways of the elk. Ronnie's new horns were starting to grow again, and he wished for a set like his father had. He would frequently visit the mineral licks that seemed to keep his feet, bones, and horns strong. One day, when he was at the mineral spring, his father was there too. They were both thinking the same thing: they were going to need a good strong set of horns to defend themselves this fall.

One day, there was a new sound down in the valley. It banged and roared and smashed down trees but showed no interest in the elk. But it was something that they kept a close eye on. Then there was a smaller thing that moved along much quieter and little things that would walk all around. To this point, they had no reason to be afraid of them as long as they stayed down in the valley.

This went on all summer, then the rut started and the valleys rang with the bugles of the elk as they challenged and defended their herds. Ronnie had a nice set of four points, and he was proud. His dad had six, and they were wide and big, and he had his ivory tips all polished up. His neck, like Ronnie's, was swelled for the rut, and Ronnie admired his father so much.

Ronnie had a dozen cows that roamed the high peaks all summer with him, and he brought them down to the big ridge that he shared with his father last year. But this year was different. When Ronnie brought his cows and calves with him, his dad started to smell them, and Ronnie took offense to it. When he told him so, his dad displayed his supremacy, and Ronnie knew it, so he took his cows to the far end of the ridge. And his dad just watched him go.

It was not long before he was challenged again and the intruder demanded his little herd. Ronnie answered that challenge, and the fight was on. Ronnie beat him up real good and drove him off the ridge right into the timber. While he was there, he stole one of his nice-looking young cows that did not have a calf with her. When she protested, he would use his horns on her to let her know that he was now boss. At the other end of the ridge, there were a lot of bugles and threats, and Ronnie wanted to go and help his dad, but every time he would start to leave, a challenger would move in to try and steal some of his cows. He took his cows and moved them onto lower ground, but he still had to fight for them. He was so busy trying to look after his herd that he did not smell the scent of his most-feared enemy.

The hunter sneaked in and shot one of Ronnie's young females, so Ronnie took them back up the mountain to where he could see better. He hoped that was the right decision, and it seemed to be better because he could even see when another challenger was trying to steal some of his females. He could go down and drive him off.

Life was one big challenge during the rut. Everyone wanted to steal his cows from him. When the rut was over, he met up with his father, who was limping quite badly. He had been gored in the shoulder and was going back to the place where he could just lie around and heal his injuries. Ronnie himself had lost a lot of weight and could use some rest, so he decided to go along. They were going through some old stands of timber and Ronnie was following his dad when, all of a sudden, his dad let out a loud snort. He was not quick enough to jump out of the way of a large male cougar that jumped on his back and was trying to bite him on the spine. Because of his stiff shoulder, the cougar would have killed him had Ronnie not jumped and gored the cougar and threw him right off onto the ground. He then stomped him to death with his front feet.

They did not go too far when Ronnie's dad wanted to lie down, as he was injured quite badly. There was not much to eat right there, so the next day Ronnie, looked for a better place, and after he had eaten, he went back to see if his father could follow him. His dad was standing, but he was so stiff that he could only walk for a short ways, and then he would have to rest. When they got to the little stream, his dad drank real long and deep.

On the other side of the creek, there was a lot of swamp grass and willow, so they decided that they would rest there. It took a long time to heal the injuries of Ronnie's dad, but eventually, he was able to paw for the grass that was under the snow, and that helped to free up his shoulder and back. The exercise was just what he needed.

It sure felt good when Ronnie's horns shed. He didn't have all that weight to carry around, and it made it easier on his neck. Then those noisy machines came back into the valley. It made Ronnie nervous, so they decided to move to another valley. When they got there, they found four elk. They were bulls that they may have done battle with during the rut, but now they would become old buddies.

The machines that came back into the valleys were affiliated with the exploration for oil. They were going to be making miles and miles of trails so that the seismic companies could do their drilling and detonating of explosives to determine what the rock formation was like thousands of feet below the surface. Oil is found in certain rock formations, and when they find the formation that they think oil could be in, they bring in a wild cat rig and drill into the formations, and after doing a lot of testing, they can determine what is down there—oil, gas, or nothing. Nothing is considered a dry hole.

If oil or gas is found, they are capped, and more holes are drilled. Then a gathering system of pipelines and roads are made, and the oil is piped to separating plants where the impurities like saltwater are separated and disposed of. If gas is found in large volumes, it has to be separated and piped into a separate system, or if the gas is of a lesser amount, it can be burned off in what is known as a flar; it is piped to a tall pipe that stands off by itself, and the gas is lit and burns on a continual basis. This all requires a lot of development, roads, bridges, and traffic, and in prime wildlife, habitat can be disturbing to the wildlife. But as the saying goes, as the world turns, it is money that greases the wheel. Many animals have been killed on roads, and when the season was opened for hunting, the wildlife was not used to the changes, and they were slaughtered. Hindsight is a wonderful judgment, but once you are dead, you are a long time dead.

The manufacturers of rifles, scopes, and rangefinders all encourage the hunter to take advantage of the animals, and in his nakedness, the animal is at a terrible disadvantage. Then to really confuse them, we let them live in our parks and teach them that man is something to be friends with so we can take his picture, but when he steps over the line, it is legal to kill him. Somehow there seems to be a bit of an imbalance to the scale.

One fall day, a truck that had being watching the herd of elk all summer drove up. Two men got out and set up their tripods, used a rangefinder to calculate the distance, and shot Ronnie's father and another mature bull from away down in the valley.

From that day on, Ronnie never trusted man and considered him his worst enemy. He took his herd and all that would follow him and went back into the mountains, where there was no development and man.

But the new development brought many more hunters into the Rockies in search for trophy heads of elk, moose, sheep, goat, bears, and cougars. And word soon spread that the place to go was into the Rockies.

Ronnie had two good years away back in the mountains and gained the respect that his father had before he was killed. In his veins ran the blood of a royal monarch. His bugle was louder than any other elk in the mountains, and his challenge was feared by all who had any intentions to steal any of his cows. He was proud of his sons and daughters. And when he would stand on a mountain and look over the valley below with his magnificent royal rack of horns, he felt like a king. He had learned to respect other animals but would fight them if he had to.

But man was an enemy that he had not yet figured out, and they were deadly. In all the times in his life that he was threatened or the times he watched his father and siblings be killed, they never once challenged him, and yet they were so deadly. He had no defense against them. He had fought the wolf, cougars, and grizzle bears but could not figure out how to fight man. And that troubled him. It was more than two years since he had any contact with them, and he was happy for that. Life was good. Sometimes the deep snow made it harder in the winter, but in all, they had coped quite well.

The mountains that he moved his herd into were quite a bit higher than where he was born and raised. In the winter, the snow would get quite deep, but the slides and south slopes would blow off and they would share them with the sheep. This country was home to herds of bighorn sheep. And like a royal elk, there were trophy rams that displayed full curl horns of forty to forty-one inches. And in their rut, they bang horns to display their superiority.

When Ronnie first heard them, he thought that man had found him and was shooting at his herd. This winter, the snow was quite deep in the valley bottoms, so the elk all moved up to where the sheep were feeding on a big slide. The snow pack was a lot deeper that winter, and an exceptionally strong warm wind caused it to break loose, and thousands of tons of snow came sliding down in an avalanche and swept everything clean down into the timber.

Many of Ronnie's herd, along with several sheep, was buried under tons of snow. The wolves, coyotes, wolverine eagles, ravens, and grizzlies would feed on them next spring. Ronnie's mom was one of the ones that were missing. He saw her trying to make it to the side of the slide, but she didn't quite make it. It was an awful thing for him to witness. He was on his own now. Both of his teachers were gone, since this last experience took his mother.

Could there be any more? he wondered as he looked at the mass destruction that the slide made. He took what was left of his herd and moved to another area that was not a slide but sort of a plateau where the wind had blown the snow off the mountain. It was a big area, and they would have more than enough grass to feed them until the new grass came in the spring.

He explored the plateau, as it was huge and had big outcrops of rocks. He liked it and thought what a wonderful place this was going to be to graze in. It had lots of water that come from the snow that melted and made little streams that found their way to the bottom of the mountain. There was a place where the sheep had a lick, and that would assure him that he could keep his horns and bones strong. His herd was smaller than it had been for a long time, but he would find more cows in the valley.

He had shed his horns and was well on his way to growing a new set. In fact, they were full grown but still in the velvet, and he was very pleased with them. They were a little bit taller, and the last two tines were a bit longer. He used the mineral lick often and felt proud of his body; he felt strong, and those horns were the best that he had grown yet.

He went down into the valley and visited with other elk and was pleased to see that there were that many and they had wintered well. He was on his way back to the plateau and was on the bench below the plateau on a bench that was the transition point between the alpine and the timber. On this ridge were a lot of poplar trees, and they seemed to grow in long thin lines along the ridge, and water seeped out of the ground all along them.

In reality, it was where the coal seams came to the surface and oxidized, and the water seeped to the surface following the coal seam. This made for excellent elk country.

He was just entering the last poplar ridge when he heard this god-awful noise. At first, he could not tell where it was coming from as it echoed back and forth across the valley. Then he realized that it was coming from up above him, and it was close. He stood in the poplar, partly under cover, and watched.

He watched as a helicopter landed and two men got out and unloaded their camping gear, which they would need for a weeklong sheep hunt. The helicopter would come back in a week and pick them up. When the helicopter lifted off, one of the men did a half circle over the poplars and that spooked Ronnie. When he ran, the pilot spotted him.

When he came back, he told the guide that he had seen the biggest elk in his life. The hunter said he would come back next year and hunt elk. The hunter got himself a nice trophy ram that placed well in the boon and crocket record book. He was an oil man, rich enough to afford a helicopter to fly him to where the game was.

Ronnie thought this whole noisy contraption was something to do with man; it just had to be. Just when he found the most perfect place to live, what should come along but his most feared enemy: man. He listened to the helicopter leave, and when all was quiet, he walked back to the edge of the poplars to have another look. All was quiet and peaceful, but he could not make himself walk back up that plateau. So instead he walked along the edge of the poplars, and after he had gone a long ways, he came to the place where his herd had come running off the plateau into the poplars below. They were scared by the helicopter and had run down into the trees. They would spend the fall in the poplars where they could work through the rut. Ronnie would rub his horns, clean off the velvet covering, and then polish them till the ivory points were shiny, and when he walked down into the valley, everyone took notice of him.

The females adored him, and the bulls feared him. Many challenged him, but few really wanted to make a fight of it. When two would gang up on him, he showed no mercy, and someone was going to pay, and sometimes both of them did. But it was different working in the trees and a lot harder; intruders could sneak in and out, and it worked Ronnie almost to exhaustion.

When he found his little friend, he was so happy to see her. He nuzzled and rubbed her, and when she was receptive, he sang her a tune that only elk know.

Then that noisy machine came back again, and when Ronnie heard it, he gathered up as many elk as he could and tried to herd them farther into the timber in the valley. Then one day, he heard shooting, and he knew there were still elk on the ridge and by now some may have even gone back to the plateau. But he was not going back.

Then he heard the helicopter come back again and wondered if they were leaving for good. The rut was almost over, and they could winter in the valley if they had to, but the deep snow and wolves could also be a big problem.

Back at the ranch headquarters, the cowboys were busy gathering up all the park horses and trailing them back to the Yaha Tinda Ranch, where they would spend the winter. They had trails from each park, and some of them were quite long, and the cowboys would have to camp out under the stars and swim rivers to make it back to the ranch. This all had to be done before the snow came, or at least before it got too deep for the horses, and nearly every year, there would be trips that were spent trudging through the snow.

The horses that were brought in early would have their shoes taken off and have their feet trimmed given a shot of dewormer and turned into a meadow to fend for themselves And so was the procedure for each group of park horses. After the horses were all gathered up from the parks, two cowboys would stay at the ranch and look after the horses. They would make sure that any that were getting too thin would be brought in and fed hay that had been hauled in during the summer. The other thing they had to keep an eye on was that the wolves didn't get too friendly as they sure love horse meat.

It takes a special person to do a job like these cowboys do. They are snowed in for most of the winter, with only an occasional visit by helicopter when they bring in supplies. They have a cabin at the corners where the Dormer and the Panther Rivers meet. There is a corral there where they can overnight if they have to and have some place to keep the horses.

These cowboys learned to like and dislike elk. In the summer and fall, they like them, but in the winter, they make a real nuisance of themselves when they come in to the haystacks by the hundreds and do a lot of damage. On their travels along the many trails they travel, they have seen many magnificent animals, and Ronnie was one of the most magnificent.

He was spotted once on the other side of the Panther River and no doubt has left a little of his genes in that area as there has been some royal bull elk in that area after his spotting.

Just east of the corner cabin, there is a big bald mountain that is called Ji Hill, and it has now been a victim of coal testing. There was a day when several hundred elk would winter on it.

When wildlife habitat is threatened, animals will react, and their reaction can cause overgrazing, which causes starvation; overpopulation, which causes disease; just to mention a few of the negative things. When animals are free, they will find what serves them best and what keeps them healthy. When animals have to worry about survival, they don't pay attention to reproduction like they normally would. When there is an open hunting season on animals during breeding season, they are more vulnerable to be shot. And not all animals even get bred.

We don't have a season on our grouse, ducks, and geese when they are breeding, do we? We don't kill our best breeding bull in our herd of cows and then wonder why our calf crop is poor or half of what it should be. When animals are harassed by man, they become vulnerable to other predators, and their numbers go in a downward spiral.

Blanket policies don't work. Each area is unique in its own way. Lack of precipitation can have dramatic effects on a given area; what works in one may not work in another.

Ronnie decided to stay in the timber and take his chances with the wolves rather than with man. He was on a scouting trip to find a place where the snow was not so deep so the herd could feed without working so hard. He found a trail that had been used before this last big dump of snow. He followed it for a long ways, and the farther he went, the less snow he encountered. So he stopped in a meadow and filled up on some good meadow grass then he walked to a nice big spruce tree and bedded down for the night.

The next day, he would walk back to the herd and bring them possibly even farther than he had gone on the trail, and then he would find a good meadow and they would spend the winter there. He had walked a long way, and it was then that he realized he had been walking downhill because going back was a lot harder going.

It was about midday, and he was in a long swampy meadow with a lot of trees in it when he heard the first wolf howl, and it was close. Then there were more that answered him. Ronnie had two things he could do: to run was what first came to mind, but he knew he could not outrun them. Once on his trail, they would keep following him until they played him out, and then he would not have enough energy to fight them.

So he decided to stay and fight. What he did not know was that there would be so many. As they approached him, he let a big snort out of him and swung his horns back and forth. But they just circled around him and sat down. Then the two alpha wolves moved in closer, and one made an attempt to come at his head while the other one tried to come from behind and hamstring him.

He charged the first one and gored him real good. But the one that was at the back of him got a piece of his leg as he lashed out and kicked it on the side of his head and broke his jaw. Then the others moved in, and they were all too close, but not close enough to reach them with a kick. If he tried to charge them, the ones from behind would jump in and try to pull him down. They snapped and snarled at, him but he did not panic and waited his chance. Finally one moved in to grab his hind leg, and he kicked him so hard that he broke its front shoulder.

Another had him by the front shoulder, so he swung his horns and pinned it, but another one had him by the flank. Ronnie kicked him off, but he was not killing any of them: they were just coming too fast. Then two of them charged in to grab him by his head, and Ronnie drove his horns right through one of them.

Ronnie knew he was going to lose the fight; there were just too many of them. They had him bleeding from the flank, his front shoulder had a gash on it, and his hind legs were both bleeding. Still he was not going to run; he would fight until they pulled him down.

Then one tried the front shoulder again, and Ronnie broke his back with his front leg. Suddenly the strangest thing in Ronnie's life happened to him; he had been so busy trying to defend himself that he never seen the man standing not more than fifty yards away, but he sure heard the shooting.

And at first he did not know where the shots were coming from, but he saw wolves fall down. He would trample them, and then the wolves were starting to run for the bush. That is when Ronnie noticed the man, his enemy.

Tom Denny was standing in front of him. Tom fired two more shots, and a big black wolf fell dead. Ronnie realized that he was not shooting at him, but he could not make himself stand there any longer, so he ran for the bush. When he reached the first few pine trees, he stopped and looked back, and Tom was just standing there looking at him. As Ronnie ran off, Tom told himself that he had saved a real royal king.

Tom was coming back from Banff with a string of horses when he heard the wolves howl. Then he saw where some crossed the trail. They were howling all around him. At first, he thought they were going to attack his string of horses, but then he heard them attacking the elk. It was then that he decided to even the playing field and help the elk out. He could not believe what he was looking at; there was this big elk, and more than a dozen wolves were trying to pull him down.

The elk had already killed a number of wolves, and there were wolves limping around on three legs, and that was when Tom had started shooting, knowing he was so close to the fierce scene he was able to save the courageous elk's life. It never stopped fighting when he shot the first wolf. The elk jumped on it and trampled it right into the ground. He was one pissed of elk at them wolves and was determined to kill them all. But he knew they would have killed him had he not come along. He didn't think he would live to see another elk with as big a set of horns as he had. And boy, did he know how to use them. He was so mad at those wolves that Tom didn't think he even heard him shoot until he'd killed the second one. When he'd shot the big black wolf and the others all made it into the bush, the animal had looked at Tom, and he wasn't not too sure if he wasn't thinking of taking him on. But he ran to the bush, and when he got there, he stopped to take one more look at his rescuer. Maybe he was saying thank-you.

Tom just dragged the wolves under a spruce tree and took a tarp and put it over them then kicked some snow on it to hold it down. It was too late in the day, and he didn't think he could have skinned them all before dark, and he didn't want to spend another night sleeping under the stars. So he went on to camp.

When Tom got to the ranch, Jay was just starting supper. Tom said, "Jay, I am going to put the horses in the corral as I have to go back in the morning and pick up my wolves. Jay, you would not believe what I saw today: a bull elk with the biggest set of horns that I have ever seen. There was a pack of wolves trying to pull him down. There must have been more than a dozen of them. He had killed a few of them and had some quite badly injured, but they had him tore up pretty good, so that kind of evened up the playing field. I shot four, and he killed four. There was no way I was going to be able to skin that many before dark, so I just threw them in a pile under a spruce tree and covered them with a tarp. I will go back and get them tomorrow. You can tend to the horses, and when I get back, I will give you a hand with the horses."

In the morning, Tom was up early and had his horses saddled and on the trail before the sun came up. He had skinned wolves before, but not that many. What he had neglected to remember was that they may have frozen overnight, and if they did, he would not be able to skin them. He should have taken another pack horse with him because there was no way he could pack them all whole.

When he got to the wolves, it was 10:00 AM. The first thing that he did was to see if they had frozen. He was relieved to find that by covering the tarp with all that snow, it had really insulated his cash. He built himself a fire and started skinning; by 2:00 PM, he still had three wolves left to skin. He put the skinned ones in the pack boxes and packed the others on top and strapped them down then threw a diamond hitch over it all and started the long ride back to the ranch. As he started back down the trail, the wolves started howling. It was kind of nice to hear them, but when you know how ferocious a killer they can be, you don't want to see them in too big a number. He got to the ranch as his partner, Jay, was getting an armful of wood for the heater.

Jay said, "If you like, just unload them here. I will pack them in for you while you attend to your horses."

When Tom took the tarp off, Jay said, "What the hell. Did you do shoot some more?"

But Tom said, "No. There was more skinning than I realized, so I brought you a few to practice on."

Tom had asked Jay to make stretchers, but Jay only had four made because that was all the boards he could find.

When Tom came into the cabin, he said, "What's for supper? I'm starving."

"Well, that's good, because I'm starving too," Jay said "And seeing as you are the better cook of the two of us, you can start supper, and I will sand down these stretchers."

Jay looked at Tom and said, "What the hell did you shoot so many for? We will be a week cleaning these things up."

Tom replied, "I didn't. That elk killed more than half of them, and that's not all. There are at least two or three more that will surely die later. Jay, I know you don't believe me, but that elk was a real killing machine, and he had a real mad on for those wolves. You better come and get it before I feed it to the dog. After supper, I will have a go at them while you are doing the dishes."

"Oh, thanks," Jay said. "I knew there was a reason for bringing Rover along. He is the best potlicker you ever saw."

Tom just looked at him and said, "You are hopeless. You will never find a wife with that attitude."

Tom went to skinning the rest of the wolves. After Jay had finished the dishes, he started to fit the hides on the stretcher boards. He asked Tom what he was going to do about the big hole in the one wolf, and Tom said, "Oh, just leave that, and I will sew that up."

He had several to sew up. One was the one that Ronnie had gored in the ribs. When they were all done, they had a real good bunch of wolf pelts.

Jonny Rivers stopped in on his way back to his trapline, and when he saw the pelts, he said, "If you give them to me, I will sell them on my trapline number for you for half."

Tom said, "I will give you three, but the rest I am going to take to Jasper to sell."

Jonny said, "Okay, we will see who will make more money."

The next year, Tom took them into a store in Jasper and offered them for sale for two hundred and fifty dollars, but they did not sell.

Jonny said "See? I sell them better. I get eighty dollars."

But Tom said, "Not so fast, Jonny."

The storekeeper said, "I want too much. They are not even tanned."

But the next year, Tom made a sign that read "These are the enemies of Ronnie Royal, Your King" and put them in a different place in the store and sold them for five hundred dollars apiece. He had a few pictures that a lady had taken of him feeding Ronnie the salt block, and the one when he was walking down Main Street blowing his bugle with his ladies. And the tourists just gobbled them up.

Ronnie only went a mile, and then he lay down in the snow to stop the bleeding. The gash on his right front shoulder was the worst, but he would heal in time. He did not feel like a beaten warrior; he felt like a battle-hardened king. He had been in the fight of his life, and he survived. There were a lot of dead wolves, and some that would die later. He could kill his enemies, but he could not kill them all, and the enemy that he thought was his worst had actually saved his life. Credit for the fact that he was standing here today had to go to Tom. He would have died if not for him. Then when the fight was over, Tom could have killed him, but he did not. Ronnie had stood before his enemy closer that day than ever before and was still alive, and that was something he could not understand.

But what else Ronnie did not know was that Tom had a change of mind, and that day, Tom had come to realize just how hard it was to be an elk and survive in a wilderness. A wilderness that was changing, and man was the reason it was changing. Tom no longer gave out information as to where the biggest rams were or where the big royal elk was ranging.

Ronnie came to the conclusion that he could bugle so loud that it would echo back and forth across the valley; he could stand tall on his mountain and proclaim that he was king. But that would only get his head on some hunter's wall, where he would be a dead king, or he could learn from all his instincts to avoid man and live in a wilderness that is no longer free.

He did not take his herd down the trail to the meadow. Instead he took them back on to the plateau for the rest of the winter. As summer came and when fall turned into the rut, he would go deeper into the valley to avoid man until the snow got too deep, and by then, man was usually not that big a problem and he would go back to the plateau.

The sheep, on the other hand, can flee higher up the mountain and can sometimes elude his followers. But with all the modern technology, the hunters usually win out in the end. One would think that living that high up you would be free of predators, but the eagle, cougar, wolf, and grizzly are all predators of the sheep and goat. The eagle is a big threat to them when they have their young. He will swoop down and knock a lamb off a ledge, and by the time it has gone down a thousand feet, it is well tenderized. They will go down and feed on it and pack the rest to their nest to feed their young.

The grizzly will feed on carrion but prefers roots, berries, ants, and smaller rodents. He also kills a lot of moose, caribou, deer, and elk calves. He is an avid fisherman, especially on salmon streams, but can kill a full-grown moose, caribou, or elk if he sets his mind to it. He also feeds on the kills of the avalanches. In the spring of the year, he can be found on the slides feeding on the new tender shoots and grasses.

From that time on, Ronnie played peek-a-boo with man. He avoided contact with him at all cost because some would befriend you, but others would kill you. He learned to always keep some cover between him and them. In the timber, he could outsmart and outmaneuver man. But when he was away up on that plateau and a long ways from them, they could still kill him. As long as he could avoid man, life was good. But he had sired so many sons, and they were now challenging him for supremacy, and he knew the day would come when he could no longer reign as king of the mountain. But until that happened, he would still blow his bugle.

There is an old story that has been told around the campfires by the old Indians and has been passed down through the ages. Jonny Rivers said to Tom as they sat in the bunkhouse by the heater that had red tinges on both sides, "Have you heard it?"

"Okay," Tom said to Jonny. "Which BS one is this one going to be?"

"No, Tom, this is true. And you should know it so you can pass it down too. Long, long time ago, there was this young boy, and he was fishing by the river, and this real big eagle swooped down and picked him up. And the boy said, 'Hey, what are you doing?' And the eagle said, 'I am going to take you to my nest and feed you to my chicks. They are really hungry, and I can't find enough food to keep them from starving because your people have killed all the fish.' The boy cried, 'Oh no, don't do that! You see, if you take me back to the river, maybe I can help you.' But the eagle said, 'I have heard that before, and I don't believe you.' But the boy said, 'Honestly. See, it is like this: if you feed me to your chicks, they will be hungry again, but if you take me back to the river, I have four fish there. I will give you three, one for each chick, and I will give the other one to my little brother because he is hungry too. And I can get you more fish tomorrow.' The eagle thought for a while and said, "Okay, it is a deal, but you have to promise me your people will stop killing all the fish, or we are all going to starve. You have to let some go up the river to spawn so there will be lots of fish for everybody. The bears, the ravens, the mink—we all eat fish." The boy promised he would. So the eagle took the fish and thanked the boy. The next day, the boy was by the river fishing but only had two fish when the eagle came. The boy was so scared that the eagle might take him and feed him to his chicks, so he said, 'I am sorry. I have only two fish and have been fishing nearly all day, but you can have them both.' But the eagle said, 'No, that would not be fair. You take one, and I will take the other one. And let some go up the river to spawn.' So the people learned to share the fish with the animals, and there was fish for everyone."

Tom said to Jonny, "That is the first story that you told me that wasn't full of BS."

And Jonny said to Tom, "Go tell your people they need to share all these mountains and rivers, the berries, the mushrooms, the trees—all the things that the Great Spirit gave us along with all the creatures on this earth."

And Tom said to Jonny, "You come with me, and we will go and tell the people in the big house in Edmonton and Vancouver and everywhere what you just told me, and maybe we can help all the creatures of the wilderness."

They did, and did it so tirelessly until they got the people to listen to them, and as a result we now have rules and regulations that have some concern for the creatures of the wild.

Jonny was a native Indian that would stop in at the bunkhouse at the ranch just to BS with the cowboys on his way back from trapping in the mountains. It was a good place to give his dog team a rest before he would journey on to the reserve at Stony. He said, "Tom, you know that the Indians were really the first people in North America, and you know why? They had reservations." And so their conversations would go back and forth, telling jokes about each other.

Ronnie continued to live his life with his many friends and offspring and tried to pass along the knowledge of the danger of man. Those that did not listen suffered the consequences. As for Ronnie, he wished he could just go over the mountain and be free of man forever. But then there were times when he had met Tom when he was leading a big string of pack horses, and Ronnie's sense of smell had failed to separate the scent of man from the overpowering scent of horse. Tom would watch as Ronnie would run for cover, where he would stop and watch Tom go by. Tom would say, "That's right, boy. You just keep your guard up, and you will live to be an old man."

But Ronnie was confused. Tom acted like he wanted to be friends with Ronnie, but Tom was a man, and it was a man that killed his father. He wondered if all men with horses would be safe to trust. He really wanted to be friends with Tom; he had a special thank-you that he would have liked to deliver but somehow could never convince himself to lowering his guard that much.

The pressure was building, and Ronnie had been seen, and the word was passed around, and hunters from all over North America sought his head just to hang it on their wall. Whenever Tom was asked about him, he would say, "Oh, he has probably gone to elk heaven by now." But then one day, Ronnie was spotted by some oil men from a helicopter just before he made it into the cover of some poplar trees, and there was no doubt that it was the royal king.

The word spread like wildfire that he was still alive and was just as big as ever. Ronnie changed his thinking and would take his herd to the highest mountain that still had a good covering of evergreen, and he would spend the rut up there. He had never experienced man up there, so felt that it was relatively safe. And it had been for the past few years. But he kept his guard up, and it seemed to pay off.

Then when he was beginning to think he had found the secret to avoiding man and where he could once again blow his bugle as loud and mighty as he once did, his world came crashing down on him.

The fall had been exceptionally mild, and the elk were still up high, and that made for hard hunting. There was a small camp of three hunters that made their camp on the Panther River, and they were using horses to hunt with. They had ridden many miles and saw a lot of elk but mostly immature bulls and cows. They had been up on JI Hill and to most places that they could get to with horses. One hunter was an experienced horseman and wanted to tackle this big timbered mountain. There had to be some big elk here somewhere in these mountains. But his partners said that was where they were drawing the line. There was no way they were going to take their horses up that steep mountain.

The one hunter said, "Why don't you and I try it on foot so early the next morning?" All three of them crossed the Panther and rode to the base of the big mountain, but when they saw how steep it was, they decided to hunt the river flats. But this energetic hunter decided he was going to give it a try. So he tied his horse, loosened the cinch, and started his climb.

He had not quite made it to the top when he came across some unusually large elk tracks in the snow, which was eight to ten inches deep. He knew that this was a large elk. He followed the tracks until he came to a spot where the elk urinated in the snow and then walked over that spot. He knew he had a large bull elk. He knew he was too late to finish the hunt that day, so he decided he would come back the next day, and he was excited. As he made his way back down off that mountain, he knew daylight was going to elude him. Because he was on the north side of the mountain, it got darker a lot quicker, but he had no fear of getting lost. When he got to his horse, it was real dark, as the moon was behind a rather large cloud. He just let his horse find his way, but soon he realized that they were going in the wrong direction, and what his horse was doing was following the other horses' tracks. That would get him home, but it might take a long time. So he turned his horse north and hoped to find the Panther River, then he would ride his horse west along the river till he came to their camp.

He found the river and turned west, and soon the horse found a good walking path to walk on. He could not believe how warm it was. As he rode along, he kept thinking of how he could get his horse up that mountain. Then the moon came out from behind the clouds, and it was like someone had turned the yard light on. How good it felt to be riding his horse out in the mountains on such a beautiful night. He was almost at the camp. As he glanced at his watch, he saw it was 9:00 PM. Then his horse stopped and looked into the river, and there stood what he first thought was an elk. Because he had elk on his mind, the hunter was fooled. It was just a buck deer but a big one. The deer was standing in the river, and in the moonlight, it looked a lot bigger. The hunter slowly slipped his 25-06 out of the scabbard and made a perfect kill.

Then he rode to the crossing and told his partners they should bring a flashlight as he had a deer down in the river. He rode his Appaloosa into the river, and when he found the deer, he dropped a loop around his horns, snubbed him up close, and dragged him back to the crossing, where dressed him out then pushed him back into the river and flushed him clean.

They threw him across the saddle, and that Appaloosa walked him right to where they could hang him in a tree. His partners would have something to do tomorrow because he was going to get him a big elk tomorrow. He rubbed his horse down, fed him some grain and some nice timothy hay, and then went in to have some supper.

As the hunter ate, he told his buddies of his plans for tomorrow. He packed him a lunch for tomorrow and planned to leave an hour before daylight. He was up early, made his bacon and eggs, saddled up, and was on his way. He found a trail that would lead him up to the top of the mountain, but in places, it was so steep he got off his horse and hung on to its tail and let the horse help pull him up. The horse would stop and rest, and then when he got his wind, he would go again. The hunter didn't know who made that trail, but it sure was a steep one.

When they got to the top, they were both huffing and puffing. His horse was really lathered up, so he gave him a good rest. When they were well rested up, he stepped up into the saddle. His plan was to just ride a big circle around on top of the big plateau. This area long ago had been burned off and was in the process of regenerating the young seedlings, which were anywhere from six to twenty feet tall. On the ground there was a lot of windfall, some two, three, and four feet off the ground. The regeneration was thick in some spots and a lot thinner in others. In some places, there were a lot of willows where the ground was wetter and kind of swampy. There were lots of feed, and the hunter could understand why the elk were up here. He was sure that he would find an elk before too long as he was seeing lots of fresh tracks.

He had shot moose right off the back of his Appaloosa and was expecting to do the same this time. He was getting to where the willows were thicker and the pine shorter and not so close together. He stopped his horse just to have a better look as he was not sure that he was able to take in all that he was looking at on the move. When he was satisfied that he had seen it all, he was ready to move on. He took his gun from the scabbard just to be sure he could get a quick shot off, if he needed to. He had only ridden a hundred yards when his horse flicked his ears ahead and was looking at the biggest elk that he had ever seen. So the hunter decided to get off his horse to get a steadier shot as he did not want to miss this one.

Ronnie had been lying down, and when he got the scent of a horse that was sweating, he immediately thought of Tom, but what would Tom be doing up here? That was when he stood up, and sure enough, there stood a horse and a rider in front of him. He stood there a little too long. The rider had time to dismount and take aim, but the little willow would be Ronnie's lifesaver this day; the bullet deflected and hit Ronnie high in the neck. Ronnie felt the hit before he heard the bang. Then the next thing he knew, he was on the ground and he could not lift his head up, nor would his legs work. He could only lie there, then he was able to lift his head, but it was so heavy he could not balance those big horns. Then he got feeling in his legs, and he immediately tried to get up. His hind legs were up, but the front ones failed to support him, and in his hurry to run, he fell on his neck. His head kind of skidded a few feet, but then the front legs were back to working again. And he just ran, but those big horns were hard to get between all those little pine trees. He was running on instinct, half blind, not really knowing what or where he was going.

As the hunter was walking up to what he thought was going to be the biggest elk he had ever shot, he just saw the back end of an elk go into the bush. At first, he thought it must be another elk, but when he got to where his elk should be lying, there was an imprint where he had been, but he was gone. There was a big patch of hair and some blood, but the back end of the elk that he just saw was his elk, and he was gone.

The hunter could not believe what had happened. He looked to see where the blood mark on the snow was, and it was in the wrong place. It looked like it was coming from the neck, and that was not where he had aimed. Then he realized that the bullet must have deflected off a willow and had just creased him.

He went back and got his horse and decided to try to cut the elk off from the direction he was going. He kept telling himself that he should have shot him right from the horse.

Ronnie was a confused elk for a little while. He could not quite figure out where he was. He knew he was alive, but his world was not standing still for him, and he didn't quite know which way to go. Then he saw the horse, so he ran, but he had to stay out in the open because his horns were so heavy to hold up and balance. This horse was running after him, and he knew he had to keep running. Then he felt a burn in his hind leg and then that awful bang.

He knew he had to keep running; that was what his mother had told him a long time ago. Then there was more shooting, and in his desperation to escape, he ran into a tree, and the horse gained on him. More shooting followed, and he was wondering if that guy was ever going to run out of bullets. They were slamming into trees on both sides of him.

Then the shooting stopped, but he didn't. That was the last time he saw the horse. But the hunter did follow him. Ronnie ran until he could no longer run then he turned around and watched his back trail. When no one came, he lay down to try and stop the bleeding in his hind leg. But then the hunter was coming again, so he got up and ran till dark. Then he lay down again, looking back on his trail. He did not rest much that night. His leg was hurting, but more than that, it was the worry of the enemy that was on his trail that kept him from relaxing and resting.

Just before first light, he got up, and his hind leg was real stiff. At first, he could hardly walk, but the more he used it, the better it got. He stopped to make a decision on what he should do or which way he should go. He stood there for a long time and just looked at the valley below him. Down there would be the ranch horses pawing in the meadow, and that would help to confuse his tracker. He would cross the meadow and climb up to the other side of that mountain, and if his leg would allow him, he would just keep on walking. He did not know where he was going, but this was going to be a journey that would take him a long ways from here.

The hunter tracked him ever so slowly, knowing that he would stop and lie down and would be watching his back trail. He didn't want to risk jumping him from too far away, and just maybe that flesh wound in the elk's hind leg would slow him up enough to get the shot he would be looking for. But when he came to where Ronnie had lain down and saw the spot that he had picked where to lie down, he knew he had an old experienced warrior in front of him. Because he had picked a spot that exposed the hunter long before the hunter would see him. The bleeding had almost stopped, and the leg was working quite well, so he had to call it a day, as much as he hated to. As he walked back to his horse, he was getting the feeling that maybe this elk was going to get away. But tomorrow, he would give it one more try.

When he got back to his horse, he was one leg-weary hunter. He mounted up and rode to the steep spot then he got off his horse and let him go. The drop-off was what concerned him the most. He really liked his Appaloosa and didn't want to see him get hurt. The trail was really not much more than a sheep path, but he was one sure-footed horse and was waiting for him a little farther down the trail. It was dark again when he got to camp, and his partners were just having their supper.

After attending to his horse, the hunter sat himself down to a good supper of potatoes, carrots, venison, and gravy. As he ate, he told them a story that he wished had a better ending to it, of how he had tried to shoot him on the run, but he said, "It is not like you see in the movies." And he sure did not want to shoot his horse in the head. He said that his horse had been jumping windfalls four feet high and not losing any ground, but it was no easy job to stay in the saddle, and there were times that he was almost a goner. It probably was a good thing he run out of shells or he may have been still lying out there on the ground with a broken back or something.

He explained to them that he wanted to walk the elk out to the meadow, and if he didn't get a shot at him, he was prepared to set him free. But that required their help. He wanted one of them to come up the mountain and bring back his horse, and then they could bring the horses down the cut line and pick him up in the meadow. If all went well, he would be in the meadow by 3:00 PM.

One of his partners agreed to give it a try. When he reached the meadow, it was twenty to three, and he was sure that they had been there, but it looked like they had gone back. That would make him at least a six—or seven-mile walk back to camp. So the hunter sat there and had a rest for almost an hour, and when they did not show up, he tried to catch one of the pack horses and was going to ride it back to camp.

But they were not to cooperative with him. The one that did not have any marks that indicated he had ever had any shoes or saddle on wanted to be his buddy. So he took his gun and put it behind his back and the strap across his chest, then he took his belt off and put it around the horse's neck and led him up to a big hump in the meadow and jumped on.

The horse took two jumps and stopped and was bug-eyed and shaking. He pet him and talked to him, and when he had him somewhat quieted down, he asked him to step up. He did it in jumps and stops. All the other horses had walked ahead of him, so he thought maybe he should follow. He did that until he got to the cut line then he turned him down the cut line toward camp. Some of the other horses thought they were going home to the ranch and followed in behind.

He went real well until he came to a little stream that had a little ice on it and was making a little noise. Then the horse made a big thing about it. The hunter gave him a little bump with his heels, and that was when he came all apart. He reared up and did an endow, and when he ducked his head, he broke the belt buckle. The hunter only lasted three jumps and was thrown over his head.

When he hit the ground, he landed on his hands and knees, but the gun smacked him on the back of the head and left him a bump the size of an egg. So now it was shanks pony all the way home. When he got to the river, he could see two guys in the tent. He called and called but could not get anyone's attention. His head was throbbing. He was tired from the long walk, and it looked like he was going to have to walk across the river.

There was going to be a change of hunting partners another year. He walked across the river and up to the tent and said, "Is there anyone alive in here?" He did not ask why they did not wait for him or tell them what happened to his elk. He changed clothes, took two Tylenol out of the first-aid box, and lay on the bed till his head quit pounding. Then he made himself some supper and went to bed. Tomorrow they would break camp and head for home.

Ronnie walked the south slopes of that mountain and came to a herd of twenty elk. They all looked at him and wondered where he had come from. There was a bull in the herd, but Ronnie was not interested in any of his cows. Then he just kept walking west. He did not really know where he was going, but he had made up his mind that it was going to be a long ways from the valley where he had been shot in.

He thought of his offspring and the herd he left behind, but he was never going back. He walked in a westerly direction down mountains, across valleys and rivers, up mountains, and he came to a big herd of elk on a big plateau. They all welcomed him into their herd and admired his beautiful set of horns. He wintered with that herd, and the winter was a mild one, so all were in good shape come spring. As the sun grew hotter, they shed their winter coats and they became shiny and slick, and all the new calves came back to the herd with their mothers.

It was good to look at, but somehow, Ronnie felt like a stranger to them. He did not know the history of their heritage like he did of the Ram River herd. His horns were growing again, but somehow he was not excited about them like he used to be. But they were a good-looking set, and he turned a lot of heads wherever he went. As the time for the rut neared, he got a new burst of life, and he would show all the bulls what a real bugle sounded like. He was still a royal king but could not defend a herd like he used to. He was not so sure of himself, but what he had was knowledge.

The younger bulls were flexing their muscles and making all sorts of challenges, but he ignored them. He would gather himself some real good cows and herd them down into the tall timber and care for them, and his genes would live on in another part of the mountains. But he could not get away without defending his little herd. A young bull that had been run off the mountain found him and challenged him. It did not take Ronnie too long to dispose of him. When he pinned him, he kept the pressure on him until he bleated. Then Ronnie backed off and stood there looking at him as much as to say, "Don't mess with the old bull if you can't stand the pressure."

They wintered well without any contact with man, and in the spring, there was a great-looking bunch of calves that carried the genes of the great royal elk. But Ronnie was restless and wanted to move on, so he left his little herd to the safekeeping of the younger bulls.

He traveled west then north and then west again. The mountains were really rugged in some places, and in others, they were easy to travel through. He came upon a small herd of just cows and calves and one young bull that reminded him of some of his sons when they were experiencing their first set of horns. Ronnie wondered where all the other elk were. In time he learned that there was a very big slide where they had been wintering, and an avalanche had wiped nearly all of them off the mountain along with a herd of bighorn sheep. So he stayed with them through the summer but did not like that area. It was too steep and rugged. He led his little herd out to where the mountains were not so steep but had more plateaus and where the grass grew better. There were mineral springs and licks, and in the valley bottoms, there were meadows that they could feed on the long meadow grass in the early winter.

By then, it was time for the rut to start, so Ronnie blew his bugle so loud that he could hear its echoes bounce back and forth from one mountain to the other. But he never got a challenge. Somehow there did not seem to be too many elk in that part of the mountains. He stayed with them through the rut and sang his little tune to all the ladies.

In the spring, he would leave the herd to the young sprout to care for them. He would move on again in a westerly direction. His horns still grew to be a good size, but they were no longer the majestic set the royal once carried. His body language was telling him that he was on the sunny slope of life. He had eluded man and was still alive, but his instincts seemed to be telling him to keep going west, so he did.

He came to a real nice big plateau, and on it was many elk. He stopped to study the situation and came to the conclusion that maybe it was a good place to spend the winter. There were valley bottoms with lots of meadow grass and a river that snaked through them. But what he didn't know was that the warm winds blew through this area and kept the snow down and that allowed the elk to do well.

He made friends with all the elk; he had lots to tell them, but he had lots of questions to ask them as well. What he learned was that there was a big valley where the grass stayed green foe most of the winter, where you could walk anywhere you wanted to and you didn't need to have any fear of man.

Ronnie said, "Look, I have probably lived longer than any one of you, and that is the reason I am here: you cannot trust man. And I have traveled over many mountains, crossed valleys and rivers just to be free of him. So I do not believe you." But he added, "I like what you told me of the grass being green all winter. You see, I am getting a little long in the tooth, and warm winds and green grass in the winter are what I have been searching for."

They said, "Come with us, and we will show you where that place is." So he followed them down off the mountain across the valley, up another mountain, and when he stood there and looked at the valley below, he wanted to run back into the mountains. There were a lot of things he had never seen before. There were trucks, cars, trains, helicopters, airplanes, lots of buildings, and people all over. There were flags blowing in the wind, lights flashing, horns honking, and all kind of strange noises.

He said, "You tell me that that is a safe place to go? Why, there are even people there."

They said to him, "You missed something. You never said you saw the green grass."

"Well, yes, I did, but there were people walking on it."

"Did you not see the elk lying on the green grass?"

He looked, and sure enough, they were, and there were others walking near the houses and the helicopter. He shook his horns in disbelief.

They said, "Trust us. We will take you there, and you can meet the elk that are there now."

So reluctantly Ronnie followed them down off that mountain across the river, past the helicopter and airplane. They were about to cross the highway, and there were cars and trucks coming, and then they all stopped.

Ronnie thought, *Now I am going to die*, but the people all got out and took pictures of him as they walked across the road. Then when Ronnie and his friends were going to walk up town on the boulevard where there was the greenest grass he had ever seen, Ronnie said, "Stop. I don't want to go there."

His friends said, "Come on. You don't have anything to be afraid of."

Ronnie was shaking worse than when the wolves were tearing the herd apart back in the mountains where he was born. But he followed the other elk. They had to cross another highway, and there was a big truck coming, but still they all walked out in front of the truck, and when the driver honked his horn, Ronnie almost bumped over the elk in front of him.

Then they walked to the big green field of grass and began to graze on it. Ronnie had never tasted anything so good before. Then they walked on to where the other elk were, and they looked at him as he was still shaking.

"Where did you come from? You look like you are really bushed."

Ronnie managed to say, "Do you really feel safe here?"

They said, "Of course. They treat us like royalty here. Relax, you don't have anything to worry about."

Ronnie asked them if they would take him back up the mountain, and they said, "Why? If any of us were as big as you and had as big a set of horns as you, we would walk up Main Street and bugle from one end to the other. Have some more of the best grass in the country."

A lady golfer started walking up to them and wanted to take a picture of all the bull elk together, but Ronnie always wanted to stand behind someone else. So one of the other bulls poked Ronnie with his horn, and because Ronnie was so uptight, he turned quickly and locked horns with him. And unbeknownst to him, that made the picture of the year.

The rut was soon going to start, and Ronnie thought that the elk would be all going back up into the mountains, but to his surprise, more elk came to town. And when the rut was in full swing, the bulls were not bashful to sing a tune to the ladies on the golf course or in front of tourists. And even Ronnie gathered himself a few special ladies to sing too, and as a result, his genes were spread from the Ram River through the mountains to Jasper Park.

As Ronnie learned to trust people more and more, Jasper felt like home to him. There was the man from the grocery store that would come out and feed him apples. He would cut them up into three or four pieces so he would not choke when he ate them. And there was a lady who would feed him plums, and she always made sure the stones were taken out first. Then there was the old couple that would buy the choicest alfalfa hay and feed him a flake from the bale every day in their backyard all winter long. They would give him salt and mineral too.

Ronnie was in the best of shape of his life. He never had anyone care for him so much before. When he shed his horns last winter, he dropped them in the backyard of the old couple that was feeding him hay, and they were as excited as two kids at Christmastime. It is not every day you get a pair of royals dropped in your backyard.

When his horns grew the next spring, they were a majestic set of royals with the top tines more than ten inches long. Once more, he felt like the majestic king that he really was. Some people called him Mr. Senior, and he would go down the streets in Jasper, and the people would come out to talk to him and give him treats.

Then one day, as he was going for a stroll to nowhere in particular, he stopped dead in his tracks, because in front of him, coming down the side of the road, was a guy leading a string of pack horses. It was Tom Denny.

As Tom came closer, he couldn't help but notice the size of this old warrior. When he was right beside him, he stopped and said, "Well, I will be dammed if this isn't the old wolf crusher himself. What the hell are you doing here?"

Tom could see the scar on Ronnie's right shoulder and hind leg, and there was no doubt that was him.

Ronnie showed no sign of fear but stood not more than two horse lengths from Tom. He seemed to be just listening to Tom as he spoke out loud.

"I am so glad to see you here. This is the best place for you. Just don't go and wander off too far when you go chasing the girls," Tom said. "I have something for you." He reached into one of his saddle bags and took out a part of an old salt block and reached out to Ronnie.

Ronnie reached out to smell it, and Tom said, "Come on, I will meet you half way." He made a couple of steps toward him, and Ronnie went the rest of the way and started to lick the salt. Tom was so occupied in thought that he never saw the lady snap the picture until she spoke up and said, "My, what a fine gesture you have just made."

Tom said, "Well, we go back a long ways."

She said, "This will make an awesome picture." She asked Tom for his name so she could send him a picture. He told her of the time he helped him out when a pack of wolves tried to pull him down in the Ram River country.

When she left, Tom went back and talked to him some more. Ronnie got to thank Tom for his help a way back in the Ram River country and Tom put the salt block under a pine tree back off the road. He wished Ronnie well, mounted up, and was on his way.

Ronnie lay down under a pine that provided a shade from the hot afternoon sun. He had a lot to digest, and it was not apples, plums, or grass.

Tom, on the other hand, was wondering what it was that led the old wolf-crusher, as he called him, to go to a place like Jasper. But he was sure he would get to live out his life and die of natural causes.

That fall, when the rut came, Ronnie took a herd of cows downtown, and he bugled for all to hear and announce that he was king. Not every town had a king, but Jasper had one. And he could sure play that bugle. When all the excitement was over, Ronnie went back to the golf course and visited with the old diehards that hadn't gotten enough of golf in the summer and were trying to get a few more shots in before the snow came. Ronnie never quite figured out that golf game. Then he visited with the old couple and other friends.

The next spring, Tom was back with another string of pack horses, and Ronnie met him just as he was coming into town. Ronnie's horns were still in the velvet and not near the size they were last year. But Tom recognized him, and this time, he shared his apple with him. Tom told Ronnie about one of his sons that was a chip off the old block and was doing him proud and how he had to look twice to make sure it wasn't the old wolf-crusher himself.

Ronnie had failed a lot over winter, and Tom noticed when Ronnie was eating his apple, he was missing a tooth. There was no doubt the years were telling the end was getting near. Tom talked to the park warden and told him all about Ronnie. He told him he was getting pretty old, and maybe they could keep an eye on him. The warden said he would, but sometimes the best thing to do was let Mother Nature take its course.

Ronnie no longer walked with the spirit of the royal king he once was. He shuffled along and dragged his legs from one step to the other. His muscle mass was half of what it once was, but he still visited the old folks for his hay and the guy that fed him the apples as well as the lady that fed him plums. He would visit with the people on the golf course; they all were his friends.

But only a few people took his picture. He did not shed his winter coat and the velvet like he normally did. His horns were not even; one side had five, the other six, but they were very uneven. By the time the rut was in full swing, he did manage to shed out, and the velvet had pretty much gone from his horns, but they lacked the polish that they always had before. Everyone knew their king was on the downhill slide and wanted to do something to help.

They wanted the park warden to do something, but he told them the same as he told Tom. They would keep a close eye on him, and if he got to a stage where he was suffering, then they would deal with it. But Mother Nature can and usually does wonders when it comes to situations like these. Ronnie made his rounds to visit with those who fed him hay, plums, and apples and then went for a walk out of town across the flats, and that was where he met Tom.

Tom fed him an apple that he had especially saved in case he met Ronnie on this trip. As he ran his hand over Ronnie's body, he knew that he would not see him again. There just was not any fat covering over those old bones, and he hoped the parting would be quick and painless.

When Ronnie finished the apple, he continued his journey across the flats and across the river and up the mountain that would overlook the valley and the town of Jasper. It took him a long time to reach the top of that mountain, and those that saw him said he rested many times.

When he reached the top, he turned and took a long look at the valley below him and the town that he learned to call home. Then he was so tired he lay himself down and soaked up the last rays of sunshine before it set behind the mountain. He knew his life had come full circle.

He was so tired he stretched right out and dosed off. He dreamed of his younger years; what it was like to get those gangly legs going all in the same direction, of his mother and how she died on that mountain in that avalanche, and his dear little friend, and his father so big and powerful. He dreamed of the time when he fought the wolves and of Tom and the special friends that they had become, the day he had gotten shot and how a little willow saved his life; how that big cat nearly killed his father; of his father's death on that big plateau. Of all his offspring that would roam through the Rockies and the ones that would become kings of the mountains. Then he dreamed of that big mountain in the sky, where the grass grows green and knee high, where the water runs cool and clear, and the breeze rustled the autumn colors. So beautiful.

Then he thought he heard his father's bugle, and as he listened, he heard the Great Spirit call, and he knew he was going home.

SECTION 2

Ferper, the Grizzly Bear

In a hole in the ground under a partially fallen fir tree is where Ferper was born. He weighed in at just less than two pounds and was about five inches long. No one seemed to even notice his arrival. But would you believe me if I told you that his mature weight was over a thousand pounds and that he stood ten feet tall?

He was conceived in a wild onion patch on a slide of a rather large mountain. And when that affair was over, he was pretty much forgotten about until the day his mother woke up in that hole in the ground. He was crawling around like a little mole and had found the fountain of life and had been partaking of it for nearly a month. Although everything was dark, he learned where the warmth was coming from and did not stray too far from it. Mainly he ate and slept until his mother's awaking. Then there was a bonding with his mother. By now, he was the size of a small rabbit with short ears and was quite capable to get around.

When he first saw daylight, it nearly blinded him because that hole had been so dark. The first few days, they did not go too far from the den, but as he got more accustomed to the surroundings, she took him farther away to where she could find more to eat.

She ate a lot of roots and grass; ants and grubs were a real delicacy. He nursed a lot and grew in leaps and bounds and frolicked around a lot. Soon he was mimicking his mother and would scratch in the ground. When he noticed little bugs, he would play with them until he eventually killed them. He chewed on roots, grass, and leaves and was soon learning to eat them like his mother.

She schooled him every day, and when he did not pay attention, she would cuff him. Life to a bear is a very serious thing; do it right and you live on. Make a mistake and you could pay with your life. So you better get it right.

She taught him all the bear senses, how to stand up to see and smell better. She taught him to listen to her and to listen for sounds of danger. If she huffed, he was to be up a tree right now. She would take care of what was on the ground. Because grizzly bears are very strong and ferocious fighters, they can and will fight most anything that threatens them. A mother bear will defend her cubs to her death. That is why you should never get between a sow and her cub if at all possible, or she just might rip you apart.

A wolf might try to steal a cub, but a mother is usually not far away and will put an end to that in a hurry. A male bear will try to kill the cub so that the sow will come back into estrus, so he can then mate with her. But she is one mean mama and can usually fight off a bore.

Ferper's taught him how to look for mice, chipmunks, roots, berries, mushrooms, and grasses, and when she went fishing and caught a fish, she would make sure the fish was still alive so he learned to kill it and eat it.

When they had lived a full summer and it was time to fatten up for hibernation, they started on berries and mushrooms and then moved on to fish to put on as much fat as they could. Then she would take him to the den or sometimes make a new one, and then they would curl up in there and sleep the whole winter.

When it came time to awake from the long winter sleep, Ferper was ready for the challenge of the outside world. He had a bit of a hard time adjusting to the bright light, but once that cleared up, he was ready for all the new experiences that awaited him. He was bigger, much more aggressive, and he was hungry. He caught the first mouse he saw and ate it. He turned over every rock that he could and looked for something to eat. Then he got the scent of some carrion; his mom was very cautious about approaching it because there could be danger there. After she was satisfied that all was safe, she took him to it. It was an elk that had been buried in an avalanche during the winter and was just beginning to show through the snow. She dug it out of the hard-packed snow and dragged it into the timber. There she ripped it apart, and she and Ferper gorged themselves. Ferper was very impressed with the strength of his mother; she could practically carry the elk over logs and windfall. Once she got it into the bush and they had gorged themselves, she covered it with dead grass, moss, sticks, and logs. Then she took Ferper to a nice mossy spot where she could see the cache, and they just lay around and digested that big meal. When they got hungry again, they went back and gorged themselves some more.

She was in the process of covering it up again when a medium-sized bore grizzly came and was going to invite him to a meal of tender elk. But Ferper's mother had news for him. She huffed at Ferper, and he scampered up a tree, then she tore into that bore. When she got done with him, he looked like a tattered old bum. As he walked away from there, he said to himself, *Boy, she is one mean old mama and doesn't have any ladylike manners at all.*

Ferper and his mother fed on that carcass a few more times. Then they went down to much-lower ground and fed on skunk cabbage, roots, and grasses. They tore old logs and stumps apart and lapped up all the ants and grubs that they could.

Ferper liked that he could test his muscles on the stumps, and he sure liked the taste of the ants and grubs. It was nice to be a bear. Most all of the other animals gave Ferper and his mom a wide berth.

Ferper liked to roughhouse with his mom, and sometimes she would, but what he really needed was a brother. Then one day, they were out in a big meadow where his mom was feeding on the nice long green grass, and another sow bear with two cubs come into the meadow.

Ferper was standing as tall as he could because he wanted to see the other small bears, and as he watched them, they were wrestling each other and seemed to be having a lot of fun. When they came closer, the mothers did not seem to be too concerned, so he sneaked out to see what they were all about. Soon they were wrestling and pushing each other around, and it sure was a lot of fun. When he had pretty much exhausted himself, he came back and just collapsed by his mom while she continued to feed on the long grass.

Then his mother let out a huff. He stood up on his hind legs to see what the danger was. Then she huffed again, and they ran for the trees. When they got there, she huffed, and he immediately went up a tree. Then she turned to face the intruder. She stood up and shook her head and made all kind of noises, but it still kept coming. Then she charged at him and tore into him and made the fur fly. But he was still persistent, and they went at it again. This time, she tried to convince him to leave, but he just backed off a little ways and sat down.

She was not a small bear; she was a good eight feet, but he was a foot and a half taller than her. He did not want to really hurt her; he was just trying to get her to be submissive. But she wanted no part of that, and her aggressiveness told him that if he carried this on, he could get seriously hurt. So he went to look for one that would like him a little better.

From Ferper's vantage point, he was so impressed with the size of that bear, and wondered if he would ever grow that big.

When his mother called him down, they went up the side of a mountain to look for huckleberries. The huckleberries were not quite ready yet, so they filled themselves up on raspberry, salmonberry, and bearberry. Then she took him to look for marmites on some of the slides. This was fun for Ferper. His mother would huff and puff and scare the marmites out of hiding, and he would try to catch them. Sometimes she would scratch and dig and throw big rocks down the mountain and catch one herself.

Then they went to the river to see if they could catch some fish. But when they got there, two men were fishing in her favorite spot. As his mother looked the situation over, one of them took a rock and threw it at her but missed. The rock hit Ferper, and it really hurt him, so he did a little bear bawl.

She immediately charged the man and killed him with one swipe of her paw. He had hurt her baby, and she was going to make him pay for it. The other man dropped the fish they had caught and ran down the trail to where they had left their pickup. She took Ferper and the fish and went back up the mountain. That was Ferper's first encounter with man, and he didn't like it because his left hind leg really hurt him, and he walked with a limp for a long time. And every time he got the scent of man, he thought of how he hurt his leg.

They went back up the mountain and found some ripe patches of huckleberries, where they just simply gorged themselves because they were so good. The berry crop was very good that fall, and they fattened up on mostly juniper and huckleberries.

On their way to the den, they came across a moose that had been very badly injured and had just died a day earlier, so they took advantage of a good situation and filled their bellies a few more times on moose meat. It looked like the weather was about to change and a storm was on its way. If it snowed, it would be a good time to head for the den as it would cover all their tracks. That is what they did. They had a bed of moss and grass, and when the door was stuffed shut with grass to keep the weather out, they curled up and went to sleep.

This would be Ferper's last sleep with his mother. When they woke from their long sleep, they had used up most of their fat reserves and were in need of food. They ate everything that they could find, but the spring was late, and the green vegetation was scarce, so they turned their attention to a moose that the ticks had weakened and pulled her down. They gorged themselves on her, and by the time they had cleaned up that moose, they could find some patches of sedge and grasses. Then they moved up to the slide areas to feed on the wild potatoes and onions and any new grasses that they could find.

Ferper was growing into a nice-looking silvertip. He could roll the bigger rocks over and look for ants and grubs all by himself. He had learned all the good edible plants to eat and where to find them. He no longer looked for the help of his mother to feed him, and he became braver to venture farther away from her. One day, when he came back to her, she had a friend with her. And as he came closer, the big bear chased him off. Anytime before, his mom would have tied into the intruder and the fur would fly.

Ferper got the feeling that he was no longer wanted, but he was a bear and a male grizzle, and he could fend for himself. He was one ridge over on the same mountain, feeding on some roots and grasses, when a big grizzle came charging and chased him off. He did not have his mother to defend him, and these guys were big, and they played real rough.

Then a little while later, he heard a real lot of growling and roaring, and it was coming from the direction of where his mother was. If she was in danger, he should go and see if he could help her. So he made his way through the shin tangle and smaller trees, and when he came over the ridge, he saw his mother just sitting there watching two real large males in a real battle for the right to mate with her.

He did not go any closer for fear that one of those big bears would come after him. He went back to looking for something to eat; he was a growing bear, and it took a lot of food to keep him full. He wondered if he would ever be as big as those big bears.

One day, he heard several shots and wondered what that all meant. Then his mother came running over to him and together they went to another mountain. She would stop and stand up on her hind legs and look back, and when she did this, the hair all along her back and shoulders would stand on end, and she would let out a deep low growl that came from deep within her chest.

He knew she had a great hatred for whatever happened back there. He was glad to be back with her. Those big bears scared him, and somehow, when he was with her, he felt safer. They roamed the mountains and valleys together all summer, and she continued to school him on all the dangers, mostly the fear of man.

On several occasions when they were at the river, she would make that deep growl in her chest. He knew it had something to do with man. They were back up on a mountain when she did that growl, and Ferper could get the scent of man. She just stood real still and smelled and listened, but the scent came on stronger. Then she made the charge.

The man had been doing some geological work for a mining company and was equipped with pepper spray and a bear banger and really had no fear of bears. However, she came so fast that he only had time to undo his pepper spray before she was on him. She ripped at and tore him apart so quickly that Ferper never really got a chance to get into the fight. Then she put her front feet on what was the biggest part left of him and jumped up and down.

When she was convinced that he was no longer a threat, she bit into him a couple more times.

Ferper looked at him and bit into him some more too. The scent reminded him of the day that the man had hit him with that rock, and he did not like him.

It was a week before anyone found the geologist, and the bears were long gone by then. They moved to another part of the mountain, but Ferper and his mother were considered very dangerous bears. They had killed a man and would do it again. When the Fish and Wildlife went out to investigate the killing, they said that to the best of their knowledge, two things could have happened: it could have been an outright attack, where the bear simply killed the geologist because he was in the bear's territory, or that the geologist had gotten between the bear and her cub and she was protecting her cub. In either case, there was not much that they could do because the trail was too old. Their suggestion was that there should always be two people, one with a firearm adequate to stop a bear at close range when in bear country, and that a person should never work alone.

The bears tried to avoid man, but man was all over in bear country, and these encounters were likely to happen if they were not made aware of the respect that they had to give the bear. Ferper and his mother stayed together through the berry season, but his mother was a cranky bear. She was always looking for danger signs and would get real short with him. Sometimes he did not want to be around her. It was at a time like this that he told himself he was leaving home and he would look after himself.

And he did; he finished the fall high up on the mountain, feeding on mice, chipmunks, picas, marmots, and juniper berries. Then the time was coming to prepare for hibernation, so he moved lower down into the timber near a big slide. He found his spot and dug a hole under some smaller trees and packed in some moss and grass. He was ready, but the weather was much too mild, so he explored the area around his den, feeding on juniper berries and a kill that a cougar had made on a caribou.

After gorging himself on the caribou, he became sleepy, and when the weather changed into a cold front that was going to bring snow, he crawled into his den, plugged the entrance, curled up, and went to sleep.

In the spring, when he woke up from his long sleep, there was still snow on the ground. So he headed for the slide and found where there had been an avalanche during the winter. Some sheep had been swept to their death and were just starting to show through the snow. The ravens and eagles alerted him to their whereabouts, and he dug them out and took them into the timber, where he would feed on them.

Then he wandered along through the mountains. His hormones were starting to kick in, and he felt like he was a real big bear, but in all reality, he was just a little over seven feet tall.

He got the scent of a female and followed her. She led him into a meadow where the grass was tall and green, and together they fed on the grass. She was a bigger bear than him but was not quite ready to be submissive yet. Then a large black bear wandered in a little too close, and when Ferper got wind of him, he charged him and overtook him before they reached the timber. It did not take him too long to kill that black bear.

Now he felt like he was a real big bear. When he returned to the female, she sniffed him all over and seemed to be pleased at what he had done. But that little skirmish left a mark on Ferper that would stay with him all his life. That black had ripped one of his ears, and it bled a lot, and even after it had healed up, it looked like he had two ears on one side of his head. Ferper and the female bear stayed together for the better part of a week, and then he wandered off in pursuit of another female. When he found one, she was a little smaller than him, and they formed a closer relationship and stayed together for most of that summer and fall.

They roamed all over that mountain, and Ferper considered it his territory. In the valley bottom, there were some nice meadows, a small river that had fish in it that spawned each spring, a small lake, a couple of slides, and a lot of alpine. It was a good place to call home. He was getting big enough to defend an area, and he decided that this was his mountain. Any other male grizzly was going to have to be a good runner or a better fighter if he was to take this mountain from him.

That summer, he had two challengers that he beat up and chased off the mountain. On his mountain, there were two sows with cubs, two younger females, and an old grandma, and that was just fine with him. He visited with them all, and they all knew he accepted them. He even took the old grandma a fish and some marmots. The last time, he sat there and watched her and wondered if possibly she could be his mother.

Another year had passed, and he was now a big bear. He was nine feet tall and weighed a thousand pounds, but that did not stop other bears from trying to come and take over his territory or claim his females. He had many battles, and some of them had long-lasting effects on him.

But like an old warrior, he fought on. He marked a lot of trees throughout his territory, and he could reach eleven feet up a tree. That told the other bears that if they planned to make this their home, they were going to have to deal with a big bear. Some came in and even took some of the young females, but any he caught had to deal with the wrath of Ferper, and usually once was enough.

One spring, the grandma bear didn't showed up. She took a long sleep and dreamed of the long journey that was before her.

Ferper was having a hard time digging a den for himself because he was such a large bear. He found a blow down at the end of the lake and made that into a real comfortable den. Things were really going good for him. He had few enemies. Sometimes he would be challenged by a young bear, but when they realized just how big and strong he was, they soon left him alone.

Then one day a lightning strike started a forest fire above the lake and burned down his house and all along the side of the mountain. However, that was not the worst thing that happened to him; when the firefighters were in the area fighting the fire, they spotted Ferper, and the word soon got out about the big bear that roamed the mountain at the little lake where the fire was. They called it Big Bear Lake even though it was just a small lake that was created by the watersheds from the big mountains that surrounded it.

The Forest Service were able to extinguish the fire before a lot of the country burned up. They used helicopters to bucket the water out of the lake and soon got the upper hand on it. When they had it contained, they put a crew of men into areas where the hot spots were. After filling up huge tubs of water with the choppers, they used water pumps connected to long hoses that were connected to the tubs and were able to spray water into the hollow logs and dead tree stumps. Then with a little spade work, they were able to completely extinguish the fire.

For a short period, wildlife habitat would be lost, but in the long run, it would be a big plus because it created so much new growth that the animals could feed on. After a fire, mushrooms of different species would grow in abundance. Bears, squirrels, chipmunks, and other birds and small animals gathered them to eat and store for the winter that was to come. The deer, moose, and elk liked all the fresh regen that came from the roots of the burnt trees and plants.

But for Ferper, it meant that a new home was going to have to be found or built. A small hole in the ground did not accommodate a bear his size; it had to be a cave. The first thing he had to find was a site that was suitable for the construction, and when that was decided on, he would get busy at it. He finally decided on a spot in the green timber about half a mile from the slide, in a stand of fir trees.

He started his excavation on a rather steep slope facing the west. The first four feet was fairly easy going. He could dig around the big boulders, and when he got them loose, he would roll them out and watch them go crashing down the mountainside. He actually enjoyed doing this. When he came to a big root that was in the way, he just chewed it off.

He could just barely turn around in his excavation, but if that big rock was out of the way, it would be okay, so he went to work at digging it out. He did not like the big hole at the entrance, so he pushed the big rock to the side of the entrance and left it there. When he went in for the last time for his hibernation, he would use it to help close the entrance.

Once he had his den ready, he could go and get something to eat; he was starving. The best huckleberry patches were burnt up in the fire, so he had to go a lot farther to find them, but when he did, he just simply gorged himself. Life was good, Mother Nature provided him with everything that he needed. All he had to do was go out and get it.

The mountains, valleys, and rivers made this place a perfect place to live, and it was his mountain and home. As he lay there in the huckleberry patch, he could hear ravens and eagles calling, so he sat up and sniffed the air to find out what they squawking about. Then he saw them circling around down in the valley, so he got up and checked it out.

Four wolves had killed a young moose, so he took it away from them. But they put up a good fight, determined to take it back. They circled round and round him, and then one would jump in and try to get a piece of him. But one got a little too close, and Ferper hit him with his swing and killed him with one swipe of his mighty paw. The others backed off and watched as he filled himself on moose meat. Then he packed the rest of it to some nice big spruce trees and guarded over it all night. He would feed on it for a few more days, and the wolves could have what was left, and that would not be very much.

He ate all the rosehips and juniper berries that he could find. He was getting fat and lazy, so he went back to his new den and packed in a bunch of moss and grass. Then he went for one more last stroll. Before he hibernated, he wanted to check his territory over one more time. Then he went back to his den, pulled the big rock into the entrance, and stuffed some moss and grass to close the hole a little more. Nature was telling him it was time to turn out the lights, so he curled up and went to sleep.

Winter was hard on the wolves. There was a lot of snow and not any real mild spells to melt the snow. Then when it freezes, they can walk on top, but this winter, it was tough slugging for them through all that snow. It was a lot colder too. A pack of them were walking along the mountainside looking for game to feed on when they happened to walk right past Ferper's den.

A little wisp of steam was coming out of the vent, and it got their attention. When they went to sniff it out, they smelled something that they thought they could eat, so they began to dig around the big rock, but they still had a long ways to reach Ferper. It was the only way that anything was going to get into the den and try to kill or drag Ferper out, but they had no idea what they were about to wake up.

The alpha male was a big black wolf and went in and grabbed a good hold of Ferper and started to pull. That woke Ferper up, but he was still in a stupor, and he was not sure what was happening. Then the wolf grabbed him again and started pulling on him. By that time, Ferper was more awake, and he reached back and got his claws around the wolf's head and dragged him into the den. One bite from Ferper's mighty jaws crushed the wolf's head. Another wolf went into the den, and by this time, Ferper turned around and reached out to get the second wolf. He ripped him apart from the shoulder to his ears. The other wolves were not brave enough to try to go into the den.

Ferper could hear them snapping and barking right outside his door. He rushed out and slapped one wolf and sent him flying into the snow. When the wolves saw how big he was, they all backed off. Ferper dragged the other two wolves out of his den and tried to stuff the hole with all the moss and grass he had, then he curled up and went to sleep again.

The eagles and ravines fed on the wolf carcasses, and when Ferper woke up, they were picked clean. The foxes and coyotes dragged most of the bones away, but Ferper sniffed the ground as he scratched around. That deep rumble that came from away down in his chest expressed the way he felt about having been disturbed in his long sleep. Wolves were not very high on his list of friends.

The spring brought animals from all over the mountains as they came to check out the burn, and some thought they would like to stay until they met Ferper. And some thought there was room enough for both of them. But one thing he knew was that there would be changes that those mountains had never seen before.

He had been challenged harder than ever, and some of them ended in kind of a mutual understanding. There were not only animals that wanted to live in the valley, but man was making their presence known as well.

Joie Ghost Keeper was one of the firefighters, and when he saw that country, he applied for a trapline there. Being he was a native, he was given the right to trap a big portion of the area. That spring, he got a chopper to fly him into the west end of the lake, and there he built a cabin.

His cabin was a crude one, but it sheltered him from the weather, and that was about all he expected. Each year he worked on his cabin and made it a little better. Ferper paid him a visit or two that summer, and when he smelled man, that deep rumble that came from down in his chest was made. But Joie would talk to him in a low soft voice and never ever made any threats to him.

One day Joie was going to the lake for a pail of water, and he met Ferper on the path. Joie was not sure that he may not have lived his last day. He had never seen a bear that huge. Joie said, "I say, sir, to him he is two time bigger me. And he just look at me. I think maybe he think I make good lunch. But I tell him I no good, fish and berries more better. But he just stand there close me. Me so scare, I just stand still, and he look at me. He make a noise like come deep in chest then he go in bush. Me go to lake get some water and go to cabin. Oh, me shake like when wind blow my panse. Me, I think maybe him like some fish. I have two nice one. I take one and give to him that one. I leave it by trail. Maybe he come and takes that one. In morning, me I go more closer that fish. He is gone. I know he come in night and take that one. It's okay, maybe he like me more better."

From there on, when Joie went fishing, he always caught one for the big guy and left it by the trail. If he snared two rabbits, he always gave one to the big guy and left it by the trail. Joie met Ferper many times after that, and whenever Joie saw him, he would always talk to Ferper, and Ferper would listen to him. Then they would go their own ways.

When fall came, Joie started to set his traps. Ferper was still around, so he would always leave something on the path for the big guy. Then when the snow came, Joie didn't see Ferper again that winter. The chopper picked Joie up just before Christmas, when he was on his way back from a mine he was servicing. He told Joie he would be coming back on the third of January. Joie asked him to bring his snow machine. He told Joie that he would.

Joie could set traps all along the lake, and he caught a lot more fur. He put bait on the lake and shot a lot of wolves. There were lots of fur, and he had a hard time to keep up with the skinning and stretching. He took all his carcasses and put them on the lake. That way, there was no mess for the bears in the spring.

When the chopper was coming out the end of February, he stopped to pick Joie up. He said he could tell what he'd been doing. He commented that it was a good thing everything was light, or he could never be able to take it all. He gave Joie a box of mothballs to put in the cabin to keep the rats, mice, and squirrels out. He asked why Joie didn't put some in his snow machine so they wouldn't chew the seat, so Joie did.

When Pat flew over Joie's cabin the next spring, he checked to see that everything was okay. On the next trip, Joie and his wife were going to come in with him. Joie wanted to do some more work on the cabin. Joie wanted to cut some trail farther up the valley to extend his trapline. When it came time to trap, his wife would help do the skinning and stretching.

Joie had his mind set on a new pickup, so he needed to catch a lot of fur. The day after Joie and his wife came to the cabin, they had a visitor. Joie had told his wife of the big bear, but now she was going to see him for herself. They got up early that morning to check out the canoe that Pat had tied to the struts of the chopper to bring back to the cabin. When they put it into the water, Joie decided they would go catch a fish. They caught four, and Joie said that was good enough.

They would give some to the big guy, who would be there soon. When they were just pulling into shore, Ferper stepped out of the bush on to the path. Joie said, "Good morning," and asked him if he'd come to get his fish.

When Ferper stood up, Joie's wife put her hand to her mouth and was about to scream. Joie told her not to make a noise, and then he told Ferper he had a fish for him, but the big bear just stood there. Then Joie told him he had some company and introduced him to his wife, telling Ferper that she was going to stay with him for the summer. Then he reached into the canoe to get a fish for Ferper, but he did not throw it at him; he made Ferper come and get it. He was only thirty feet from the canoe. He got down on all fours and came and took the fish and wandered off into the bush.

Joie told his wife they would take the rest of the fish and have one to give the big bear if he came back in the morning. She asked why he gave the bear the fish. He said it was because this was the bear's country and lake, and the bear let him come and live and trap there.

She told him she had no idea that a bear could grow so big, and she was glad when he introduced her to him, he didn't want her to shake hands with him. She asked if he was not scared to live out there when there were big bears like that around.

Joie said he wasn't, and it was good to have big friends. Joie and his wife left the fish on the path the next morning, and got into their canoe, and paddled to the other end of the lake. Then they started to clear a trail wide enough for Joie to go through with his snow machine. It was a slow, back-breaking job, but that new shiny pickup was on his mind, and he continued to work on until the job was done. They did not see that much of Ferper. He was busy defending his territory. Joie and his wife improved on the cabin and made more stretching boards so everything would be ready for the beginning of the trapping season. Then he made a hanging tree where he could hang meat to keep the wolves and wolverines from stealing it.

Pat was going to pick them up with his plane around the first of September so they could go and get their supplies for the winter. They did not plan to go out for Christmas. Pat would just take their furs in for them and drop them off and bring a little more gas back for them. They lived close to the land, so they did not need much of anything else.

Ferper had a good spring and summer. The fall was looking good too; there were lots of berries, and he was in very good shape. Then one day he heard a chopper, but it did not go to Joie's place; it went to the top of the mountain. So he thought he should check it out.

When he got near the top, he heard some shots and that did not make him happy. He remembered the time his mother came running to him that day on the mountain, and she was so angry. He knew this had something to do with man and shooting. He was nearly at the top of the mountain when the chopper came back again, and this time, he saw two men go into the chopper and they had two big sets of horns from two big rams.

Times were changing, and he did not like it. He had gone a long way to get away from man, but they just kept following him into the remote regions of the wilderness. If they had any intentions of harming him, he would treat them with the harshest treatment that he could. He roamed the mountain, feeding on carrion and rose hips. He really liked them, and when he was up high, he would fill up on juniper berries. The mushrooms were done for this year, but they were a very good crop because of the fire.

Ferper made his last round by the lake and Joie's cabin. There were a couple of skinned martin carcasses on the path, so he took them and went back up to his den.

It was getting that time. The lake was frozen just enough to go along the shore, but Joie still didn't feel safe going right across the middle. There was not quite enough snow to work the new trail yet. But Joie walked in a short way and found something in his traps nearly every time. Then they got six inches of snow, and it got a lot colder. Then he could make a set for fox, coyote, and wolverine with the carcasses and a little scent. Joie had his own formula for scent. It was one fish, one can of sardines, two beaver casters, a little aniseed oil, and meat from a coyote or martin. He chopped that all up and put it in a jam jar with the lid on tight and put it behind the stove for one week. Then it was ready to use, and the smell that you got from that would singe the hair in your nose. But the animals loved it.

Joie was a good trapper and read the signs of the animals very well. Something else he used was moose hide and grouse inners and feathers. He used the scent gland on the moose legs as bait as well. By Christmas, he almost had enough furs to pay for his new pickup. Pat stopped in and took them to the fur buyer for him. He commented on the fact that Joie had been really given it with his trapping. He kidded him about how much he was going to have to pay his wife. Joie replied that he would buy her new moccasins.

Joie trapped until February when Pat was making his run from the mine and stopped at Joie's cabin and took them and all their furs back to the little village. Joie told Pat, "Me like you, take me all time my cabin come," and he motioned for Pat to come to the house.

Pat really didn't want to spend too much time because he was on radio contact with the helicopter office, and they could call anytime. He knew if he didn't answer, they would get concerned as to where he was. But he told Joie he would have to make it a quick one. When he went into the house, Grandma was sitting in her rocking chair by the heater. Joie spoke to her in their native tongue, and she got the jacket. It was a beaded buckskin jacket with a helicopter beaded on the back.

Pat said, "Thank you, and thank you too, Grandma." What a wonderful gift. It really meant so much to Pat. When he got into the chopper, he called the office and told them he was leaving Joie's place and of the wonderful gift they had just given him.

Joie had worked for the forest service on many fires and was responsible for getting a crew of men together so the chopper could pick them up and take them to the fire. They made a spot for the chopper to land right at Joie's place. It was just a courtesy that they helped Joie out on his trips to the cabin because it was right on their way.

Joie shoveled out the old Chevy, and when he got it running, he headed for town with the rest of his furs. Then he went to the Ford dealer for his new pickup. He bought a bottle of Crown Royal and took it to the office of the helicopter company and gave it to them. He said, "Good company, good whiskey." It was his way of saying thank-you.

The mining company had got to the point where they had to make a decision as to the feasibility of building a road into the mine or to put it on hold until they could they could get more information on two other pieces of property that looked quite promising. This changed the flight plan of the chopper company and, as a result, was not that good for Joie. But the summer was a dry one, and there were quite a few fires, so they kept him busy all summer.

When October came, Joie went into the office of the helicopter company and asked them if they were going to be doing any flights over his cabin that winter. They told him they would, but they wouldn't have a regular schedule. However, if he wanted, they would see to it that he got to his cabin, but they didn't know when they could fly him out. He said if they could fly him out somewhere around Christmastime that would be okay because he had been trapping it quite hard and he could give it a rest.

The next week, they flew him in and said they would have a few trips to make in the New Year. Joie said that was good for him; he would be ready by the end of December. And by the end of December, he had all his traps and snares tripped, and he was waiting for Pat to come and pick him up.

The following fall, he had gotten in before it was time to start trapping, so he took the canoe and paddled up the river to where a small creek came into it. He beached the canoe and walked up the creek. There he found a beaver dam that he didn't know about. He checked it out and found that the beavers had made a good-sized pond and there were four rat houses and two beaver houses in it. He had some larger Kona bear traps and a few leg holds that he wasn't using, and they would work for the rats and beaver.

He paddled his way back to the cabin, where he got his traps and checked them over. He had a few minor repairs to make, and the next day, he planned to go back and set them. He had just finished splitting some fir into thin boards so he could make some rat stretchers. He was in the cabin working on the rat stretchers when there was a scratch on the door.

He went to the door, and there was the big guy. Joie's first thought was that he didn't have a fish for him. Joie spoke to him softly, saying hello to him and telling him that he didn't have a fish for him, but he had some bannock and asked him if he'd like some. He left the door open and went back into the cabin and got the bannock.

When he returned, Ferper was still standing there. Joie told him he didn't know if bannock was good for big bears, but it sure was good for an Indian. He sat on the step and broke off a chunk and gave it to the bear. Then he broke off a chunk for himself and started to eat it.

Ferper smelt it and watched Joie eating his. Then he sat down like a teddy bear and took a bite of it, and after tasting it, he ate more. Joie thought it was a good thing he had made lots that morning because that was one big guy. He thought about it and decided he didn't want to bring him into the cabin because he thought he would break his chair. After they had eaten the entire bannock, Joie told him that he would have a real treat for him the next day. He knew bears liked beaver, and he would have a good one for him. Ferper got up and burped and walked off into the bush. If you asked Joie, he would say he knew that big guy, because they had lunch together.

The next day, Joie went and set his beaver and rat traps. When he had set the last rat trap, he went back to checked the beaver trap before he went home, and to his surprise, he had a beaver in it. So he had a beaver for the big guy. He took his beaver home and started to skin it out, and when he was nearly done, who should come along but the big guy. He watched him finish skinning it, and then he gave the carcass to the big guy. He took it and left. Joie felt that the bear looked happy. A beaver to a bear was like giving Joie chocolate cake for desert.

The weather turned real cold and the lake and river froze over, so Joie was able to use his snow machine to check his traps, and as soon as it snowed a little more, he would be able to do the whole run. His trapping was really going good. He had twelve beavers, fifty rats, and four otters that were over and above all the other fur he normally caught. He was really happy and still had two weeks to go before Pat would come. He had just finished tripping all his snares and traps when he heard the chopper.

He hurried back to the lake just as Pat was about to take off again. Fortunately, Pat saw him coming across the lake and waited for him. He told him he would be back the next day and if Joie could be ready to go, he would take him and all his furs. Joie said he'd be ready.

When Pat got there the next morning, Joie was on the lake with all his furs. When Pat saw the beavers, rats, and otters, he asked where he trapped them all. Joie explained how he'd found a beaver dam on the creek and the pond that they'd created. He told him he'd trapped them there but assured him that he hadn't taken all of them; he'd left some to make more next year.

Pat had a very high regard for Joie. He might be an Indian, but he knew a hell of a lot more about the animals than any of the officers did, and there was one thing for sure: he knew how to trap. Pat really liked the otters, so Joie gave him one.

Joie told Pat that if he had a good summer, he was going to build a new house. He said the one he had was too small because he had no place to keep his furs. He wanted to make a bigger one where he could keep his fur in the basement where it was colder.

The next summer the forest service got in touch with Joie and told him that the mining company was purposing to build a road from the town to the mine. They were looking for someone local to do the slashing and burning of all the nonproductive brush. The bigger timber would be trucked out when the road was built. It was going to be a big job. Bigger than anything Joie had ever done before.

He asked them to let him think about it for a few days; then he would come back and let them know. He went to Pat, and they talked about it for several hours. He told Pat his concerns. He thought it would help him make a bigger house for himself, but he was worried it might be too big a job for him to take on. Pat told Joie to find out what they wanted done and how much they were willing to pay and then come and see him.

That made Joie feel better, and he told Pat he would go see the company the next day. When he came back, he told Pat that the right of way was to be two hundred feet wide. Pat and Joie put their heads together and estimated he would need twenty-five power saws and fifty men and several crew cabs to move the men around. Joie went back to them with a proposal for two thousand dollars a day, stating that they could expect a mile and a half a day on the flat ground. Joie's crew would slash and buck and start all the fires, then the CATs would have to push the bucked wood to the fires.

The company told Joie he was too expensive, but Joie told them he didn't want to go broke. A couple of days later, they told him he had the job. The helicopter company backed Joie on the power saws, and Ford leased him the trucks. He went to the helicopter company and asked them if they would do the books for him. They were willing to, and Joie was on his way to being a big contractor.

What Joie did not know was that the road was going to go right through his trapline and would severely damage parts of it. When he complained, the government said they would relocate him, but he declined the offer. He had made trails and built a cabin, and they would not compensate him for any of that. He knew he could not fight the government, so he said he would keep his trapline. He told Pat that maybe one day the government men would come to stay in his cabin and he would trap them.

Joie was doing very well working on the road right-of-way. It was a steady income but he had a bit of a problem with his crew. They were not all like Joie and did not care if they worked every day, so he went through a lot of men before he got a good crew.

The next summer, he hired a contractor to build a log house with a full basement. He did not trap on his line the next winter. The road went right by the lake and his cabin and from there into the big snow-capped mountains.

Ferper had made several trips to Joie's cabin, but Joie was never there, and he never found a gift from him lying on the path. The valley was changing, and he was missing Joie, and he wondered what could have happened to him.

There were men and machines all over, and Ferper wanted to leave the mountain, but he wanted to see Joie first. Maybe he could help him to understand what was happening,

Joie was a real busy man. The road was developed past his cabin, and all the slashing was finished right up to the big rocks. From there, it would require a lot of blasting as they worked their way up and through the more rugged part. There were a few places where they needed some more slashing, but they wanted to finish some of the steeper area first.

Joie was spending more time with the contractor who was building his house, because he was hoping to be in it before Christmas. If he didn't have to go slashing, he would go trapping this winter. He had a lot of work to do on his trapline because the road had gone right where he slashed his trail. He had to reset all his traps and keep them far enough from the road so no one would steal his fur or traps. He would go in early to get that done. But the big guy weighed heavily on his mind; he did not know what to do with him. He knew Ferper would be reluctant to leave the mountain, but that would be the best thing for him to do. There was just too much development for a bear like the big guy. Once he was spotted, there would be people who would be after his hide.

Joie wanted to protect him if he could. He wondered if the big guy would follow him over the mountain, and then if he did, he didn't know how he would get him to stay there.

He baked a big batch of bannock and decided to go get a fish to give him. He hoped that they could go for a long walk; he knew it was going to be risky, but he had to try. He wondered if he should have told his wife what he was planning to do but didn't think she would understand. When he was coming back from fishing, the big guy was standing on the shore where Joie beached his canoe. Joie talked to him, and the big bear just stood and watched him.

Joie was not sure what he would do if he did not give him the fish as he always had done, but he wanted him to follow him up the mountain. He decided he would go to the cabin to get the bannock, and if he could get that far without a problem, he might have it made.

When he got out of the canoe, he just kept talking to the big guy and walked to the cabin. Ferper just followed him. When he got to the door, he left it open while he got the bannock. Then he gave Ferper a piece and turned to close the door. He spoke to Ferper and said, "Let's go." But Ferper just stood there. Joie broke off another piece of bannock, reached out to him, and said, "Let's go." This time, the big guy stepped up and took the bannock ever so gently from Joie's hand.

As Joie started to walk away, Ferper followed him. They walked for several hours before Joie gave Ferper the fish. When the bear was done eating it, Joie got up, and they started to climb again.

That is when it all happened. Joie slipped and fell, and he hit his head on a rock and knocked himself out. When he came to, Ferper was licking his face. His left shoulder was hurting him badly, and he could not move it. His first thought was, *Is he eating me?* Then the big guy grabbed Joe's backpack, lifted him up, and started down the mountain. Joie said the pain was so bad he must have passed out again.

When he woke up, he was at the cabin. He thought he was dreaming, but when his head cleared a little more, he was right in front of the door. He had no idea how he got there. When he tried to get up, his shoulder and back hurt so much he thought he was going to pass out again. However, he knew he had to get up and get into the cabin. He finally managed to get to the bed and just lay there. He did not know if he passed out or slept, but when he woke up, Ferper was there and was licking his face again. It was light outside, and the door was open. Then he thought he heard a truck door slam shut.

That is when Ferper let that deep growl out of him, and Joie tried to warn whoever it was that there was a bear in the cabin. But it was too late. The CO was just coming around to the door when he ran right into Ferper. He pulled his .38 Magnum and fired at Ferper's head. The bullet went into his mouth, taking out some teeth, and came out by his eye. That enraged Ferper so much that he ran right over the CO and ripped his scalp from his ear to his chin. Then he picked him up in his mouth and shook him like a toy. When he did not move, he walked off into the bush.

Ferper's head was hurting him so bad he knew he had to get out of there. He wanted to help Joie, but they were trying to kill him. He had been wounded and had lost one eye and some teeth. He thought it best that he leave.

A driver of a company truck saw the CO's pickup parked right in the middle of the road in front of Joie's place. He got out to investigate and came upon a gruesome scene; the CO was conscious but bleeding badly, so he ran to his pickup and called for a chopper to come to Joie's cabin. Then he ran back and bandaged up the CO's head. When he had that done, he went into the cabin, and saw Joie lying there, still alive.

He had no idea what had happened to Joie. So he ran out to the truck and called for help, reporting two men badly mauled by a bear at Joie's cabin and saying they needed a chopper and medical help quick.

The office of the helicopter picked up the call and had a first-aid attendant on the chopper and on their way. Pat heard the call also; he was just leaving the mine and could be there in about fifteen minutes. He arrived first, and when he got to the cabin and saw the shape the CO was in, he asked how Joie was. He was told that Joie was awake but had to be delirious because he kept talking about a bear that tried to save his life.

Pat went into the cabin, and Joie was in a lot of pain but was not torn up. So he told Joie that the CO was badly hurt, and he was going to take him out right away. He assured him that the other chopper would take him out. He had just landed, and there was a paramedic with him so Joie would be in good hands. The CO was put on a stretcher, and they were headed for the closest medical attention. When they tried to move Joie, they knew they had some serious injuries. The paramedic got him on a stretcher and into the chopper, and then while they were flying, he gave Joie a sedative for the pain and diagnosed him to have a broken arm, a dislocated shoulder, and a severe concussion. But what he missed was the broken vertebrae.

When Pat touched down to fuel up, the decision was made to fly the CO right to Vancouver because he was in need of a lot of plastic surgery to reconstruct his face. They flew Joie to Grand Prairie, but when they found out that he had a broken back, they flew him to Vancouver as well.

The investigation team went to Vancouver to talk with the victims. They got two different stories. The CO said it was a huge grizzle that had one ear split and that there was no doubt he was a man-killer bear. He was in the cabin and was trying to kill the Indian, and when he came to the door, he charged him and tried to kill him. He had put a well-placed shot in his head; it did not have any effect on the bear. The bear had knocked him down and then picked him up and shook him like a dog would shake ragdoll. Then he had thrown him at least eight feet, and when he passed out, the bear must have chewed him up because he ripped his scalp and had several other bite wounds. When he woke up, the bear was gone.

Joie said the bear was his friend and that they had lunch together. He told them that because of the road and new development, he knew that someone would try to kill him just because he was such a big bear. So he was taking him over the mountain into another valley and hoped that man would not find him. But he slipped and fell and broke his arm and hurt his back, shoulder, and head, and he'd been in so much pain that he kept passing out.

When he came to, the bear was licking his face. Then he picked him up with his mouth and started to carry him down the mountain, but the pain was more than he could stand and he passed out. When he woke up, he was by the cabin door. He was cold and tried desperately to make it in to the cabin. He said he just lying on the bed when he got to it. Then he passed out again, and when he woke up, the bear was licking him. The door was open, and it was daylight.

Then he'd heard a truck door slam, and the bear turned to go outside. Joie told them he'd tried to tell the CO that the bear was inside the cabin. When the bear went outside, the CO shot him and the big guy chewed him up. Then another man came and patched him up and called the chopper.

He told them how the bear had come around when he'd been trapping and had never once tried to hurt him; instead, it had sought him out like a friend. He told them that the bear probably didn't like people to shoot at him, and that was why he attacked the CO.

They came to the conclusion that the bear was a killer bear and should be destroyed. They agreed to send two COs and the best native hunters they could find to track him down and kill him. They knew he would be dangerous because he had been wounded. They established a base at Joie's cabin so that they could talk to the hunters at any time.

The first day they did not see any sign of him, so they brought in two tracking dogs and combed the mountain but still were not able to find him. Then they used the chopper to fly back and forth to see if they could spot him. But that did not bring any better results. The bear had been shot in the head; maybe it had died. They called off the hunt.

Ferper had crossed the river and was less than a quarter of a mile from them all the time. When the choppers left, he went back to the cabin. He was hurting real bad, but he wanted to see Joie. Was he still alive? Or had the choppers taken him? He went to the cabin when it was dark. Joie was nowhere around; could he be inside? The door was shut, and he did not know how to open it. He scratched on the door, but no one came, so he got his claws into the crack and started to pull. It came open in pieces. He went in, but Joie was not on the bed. Maybe his friend that came got Joie with the chopper, but there were so many choppers, it confused him. He had tried to help him, and maybe someday they would meet again, but now he was going to have to leave the valley because he thought the man who had tried to kill him would come again to finish the job.

He took the same trail that Joie had led him on when they had gone up the mountain. He stopped at the spot where Joie had fallen. He sniffed all around round, and he could pick up Joie's scent, but his sense of smell was not very good now because the bullet had broken some bones in his nose. He was getting an infection, and his eyes and teeth were hurting him. He was having trouble eating; he was hungry. He stopped at the first patch of huckleberries he came to and tried to eat, but his tongue was badly cut from where the bullet had passed through his mouth. His jaw was aching where his teeth were missing, and eating was not a good thing to do right now.

So he started up the mountain again, and that was when he first heard the baying of the hounds. It struck fear in his heart; he had heard them before when they were looking for him. He didn't know if they were following him now, but as he listened, he realized they were coming closer, and he sensed that they were planning to kill him. So he hurried up the mountain.

A CO was passing by Joie's cabin and saw the door was open, so he stopped to check it out. When he realized that a bear had ripped it apart, he radioed another CO who was not too far behind him. He had a pair of blue tic hounds with him. They estimated that the trail was fresh, and from the size of the tracks, they were quite sure it was the bear that they were after. They turned the hounds loose, and they picked up the scent and went across the road and up the mountainside.

When Ferper got near the top, he could see the hounds and they were coming up quickly. There were only two, and he knew he could take care of them, but it was the men who he hated. They were the ones who would kill him. He could stay and fight the dogs and probably kill both of them, but that would only let the men get closer to him.

He decided to go on and keep as much distance between him and the men as possible. He went right over the mountain and down the other side.

The north side of the mountain had timber that nearly came to the top. He went down into the timber and found a place to rest while he waited to ambush the dogs. He had a much-needed rest and when he heard them come over the top of the mountain, his instincts told him it would not be long now before they would be on him. What he had done was go past his ambush, circle back, and wait for them. When they were just past him, Ferper jumped on the dog that was in the rear and whacked him a good one. He then charged at the other one and knocked him over. He grabbed him just behind the front legs and killed him instantly. But his jaw hurt him so bad when he bit into him that he ripped him apart with his claws until he was just pieces. The other dog was still alive, so he did the same to him. Ferper's jaw hurt him so bad that he hated man worse than ever before.

When the COs got to the top of the mountain, they could no longer hear the hounds. It was 4:00 PM, and they were tuckered out. Their feet hurt, and they decided they would not go over the other side of the mountain since they could not hear the hounds. So they radioed the office and requested a chopper to pick them up on the mountain above Joie's cabin.

The next day, they landed the chopper on the top of the mountain, and three COs and a native tracker went down the mountain to where Ferper had killed the two dogs. When the tracker saw what the bear had done to the dogs, he said that was one pissed-off bear. He told them a bear wouldn't do this to the dogs unless he was really mad. He said this was a very dangerous bear and a smart one. He told them his job ended right there because he would not go after a bear like that no matter how much they paid him. He suggested they leave him alone and let him find himself an area somewhere away out there where there was nobody around. He felt the bear would die pretty soon anyway because he was a wounded old bear.

But the department gave orders to kill him, and word was out that anyone who could kill him would have his picture on a plaque with a write-up and a story of this huge killer bear beside his mount.

Joie still was recuperating in the hospital. The CO was out of the hospital but needed a lot of plastic surgery done on his face. Pat had been in to see Joie several times, and on the last visit, he told Joie what the price was on the big guy's head.

Joie said, "They can't do that. He tried to save my life. Get me out of here, by the gee. I'm going to do something about that."

Pat cautioned him to go easy until his back was ready, and then they would do something about it.

As soon as Joie got out of the hospital, he went to the fish and wildlife office and asked them what they thought they were doing by trying to kill his friend. Their reply was the bear was a man killer.

Joie's reply was "Have you got friends?"

The officer said, "I sure do, Joie."

Joie said, "Okay, you tell me who and I'll go kill them."

The officer said, "You can't do that."

Joie said, "Oh, it's okay you kill my friends, aye?"

The office said, "But, Joie, he nearly killed you and my friend."

Joie said, "He no kill me "He save my life. He no kill you friend. You friend he try to kill the big guy, my friend. You friend try to kill him with small gun. No good. He makes him pissed off, and he chew him up, but he no kills him. I try to tell you what happen, but you think I talk crazy and you no listen me. Only white guy go kill big bear two times bigger me with small gun. He crazy. You stop telling everybody go kill my friend."

"Are you telling me that that bear tried to save your life? How did he do that?"

So Joie told him how he had made friends the big guy and how he would leave a fish by the trail for him and how he would come to the cabin and sit down outside in front of the cabin and they would eat bannock together. He told him that he knew when all the development came that someone was going to kill him just because he was such a big bear. So Joie was going to take him over the mountain and try to get him to stay where there were no people. But he had slipped, and he fell and broke his arm and back and had gotten a bad concussion. That big guy packed him off the mountain and left him by the cabin. And when Joie woke up, the bear was gone. Joie told the officer how he managed to get to the bed and passed out again, and when he woke up, the bear was licking his face. That was when the CO came.

Joie said, "I tried to tell him that there was a bear in the cabin, but he tried to kill him with that small gun and make him mad and he chewed him up."

The CO asked, "Why didn't someone tell me this before?"

Joie said, "I don't know. Maybe because I am just one Indian."

The push to kill Ferper was called off. And for that, Joie was very thankful. He could go home and recuperate. His house was finished, and Grandma thought it was too big and too fancy, but Joie's wife loved it. But Joie knew he may never trap again because his back was quite badly broken. So Joie was thinking about what he could do. One day, the thought came to him that he could build a few log cabins and a store by the lake and do business with the tourists that were coming to the lake. His wife could run it, and she could sell buckskin jackets, gloves, moccasins, slippers, caps, and all kind of Indian artifacts.

He ran the idea past Pat, and Pat thought it was a good one. Pat assisted Joie in getting the proper leases and made him aware of all the regulations that he would have to abide by. When Joie had everything in place, he started building. He got a lot of help from the other Indians to do the building. First the store, then the two cabins. He got as many of the native people as he could to make things for sale and put them in his store. He added three more canoes as a lot of people wanted to go canoeing around the lake. All the cabins were made by natives. All the furniture was made from the forest. The two cabins had two rooms with a big window facing the lake.

In the winter, he advertised cross-country skiing and snow shoeing. This was truly a wilderness retreat with no power and no noise. At night, you could watch the northern lights and stars.

For entertainment he added dog sled rides around the lake. But he needed one other thing, and that was a place to feed people. So he built a small restaurant. He got native people to cook and serve, and they did a lot of traditional meals. One that went over really big was bannock, blueberries, and tea—a traditional Indian meal.

Within a year, he had outgrown his idea and had to add two more cabins and one bigger cabin with a big living room with a big fireplace and two bed rooms. It was fully booked all the time.

Next he had to build a staff house for all the help. And by now it was looking like a small town. He called it Joie's Retreat. When he got caught up with the building, he made a big fire pit and put chairs that were built out of natural wood all around it. He called it the story pit, and in the evening, he would tell stories to the people. And the most popular one was about a grizzly bear; the big guy, as he called him.

Indian affairs helped him to fund and build a lot of it. They built a bigger restaurant, and the mine put in a big power line. Now he had power for his freezers and refrigerators. Pat helped him with some ideas and gave him pointers on various things. Pat was one of his first customers.

Joie sort of become a legend. One day, when Pat was staying in the big cabin with his family and Joie was getting the story pit ready, he and Joie were talking and Pat asked him when he was going to go back trapping. Joie just smiled at him and said, "I am trapping the tourists now."

Pat laughed and said, "You are doing a good job of it too, Joie."

Joie hung all his traps and snares on the wall of the cabin, as well as his ax and snowshoes. And that was a bit of an attraction to the tourists to see firsthand an Indian trapper cabin with all its traps and snares.

Ferper did not have a good winter. He didn't get enough fat on him for hibernation. He was having so much trouble eating from the wound caused by the shot he had received. He woke up way too early, and because of that, he was not a happy bear. The other thing was that he did not have a good den; it was just a shelter, and he was cold. There was still a lot of snow on the ground. He had never experienced a situation like this before. Wherever he looked for food, he had to dig through the snow. Then he found a carcass of a moose that had been wounded and did not make the winter. That was what saved his life, because it was still cold out, and that meant that he had to eat a lot more and more often.

He dragged the moose in to some spruce timber and scraped up a bed of moss grass and twigs under a big spruce. That would be his bed for the rest of the winter. He ate on the moose, including most of the hide all winter, and was still quite skinny and grumpy. When the snow finally started to disappear, he could dig for roots. His jaw and tongue had healed up good, but his eye and teeth were still bothering him. When he tried to crack the bones of a carcass, that side of his jaw was missing too many teeth. Then he found a carcass of a deer that the coyotes and the birds were feeding on. He chased them off and cleaned that up.

He was not a very impressive bear, and he wanted to destroy everything that he came in contact with. And he blamed it all on man. They caused him to have only one eye. They wrecked his sense of smell and to lose half of his teeth on one side. He killed other animals that he would never have hurt before. But he was mad at the whole world.

He was in an area that did not seem to have any man, and for that he was glad. He was just getting himself back together again when he was in a nice huckleberry patch one nice fall day. He thought he got the scent of man. Could it be Joie?

Then he caught the scent again and knew it was not Joie. He had no intention of leaving that berry patch. The two hunters had been hunting moose. They had ridden their horses in a long ways and did not see any moose. But when they saw Ferper and the size of him, they wanted him.

One hunter said, "You know, maybe we should just keep hunting moose."

But the other one said, "By god, legal or not, I am not passing up a chance at a bear that size."

So he went after Ferper. When he got to within four hundred yards, he took aim and touched one off. It did hit Ferper in the belly, and his roar could have woken up the dead. The hunter shot again and hit the bear in the hind leg. But that did not put the big guy down. He was trying to get to some balsam trees when the guy shot again and missed. Then he shot several more times.

Ferper made it to the bush. As he lay there, he knew he was mortally wounded, but he had not even seen the man who was shooting at him. As the hunter approached the trees, Ferper got a good smell of him and the urge to kill welled up in him. The hunter walked right on to Ferper without seeing him, and Ferper charged at him. He would have had him before he even got a shot off, but the wound in his hind leg did not give him the jump he needed.

The hunter made the shot and hit Ferper in the neck and front shoulder, but that did not stop the big guy. He was on the hunter and chewing and ripping him apart. He bit onto his face and literally ripped it off then he grabbed him by the stomach and ripped the side out of him. He continued to bite him all over and rip big gashes on his body. He broke off balsam trees four and five inches in diameter and literally ripped that mountain apart. The wound in his neck and shoulder was pumping blood out so fast that it was just a matter of minutes before he was going to be dead.

The other hunter rode his horse back as fast as he could to get to the camp where the truck was and radioed a request for a chopper for help. Pat was at Joie's place by the lake, talking to him, when he heard the call. He looked at Joie and said, "Get in. I am going to need you."

When Pat got to the top of the mountain, he called the hunter and asked for directions. The hunter gave them to Pat, and Pat told him he would be there in ten minutes. They found the camp and landed in a meadow, and the hunter came running to them. He said, "I don't think there is any use of going back there because I am sure he is dead, and I don't want anything to do with that bear. He was throwing him around like a ball."

Pat said, "Just calm down. Your partner could be still alive. Can you get in and show me where it is?"

The hunter said he would only go if they were going into the chopper. When they found the spot, it looked like a plane had crashed there. The trees were broken off, the ground was all torn up, and there were clothes scattered around and the broken and torn remains of a lifeless body.

One hundred feet from there was another lifeless body; it was Ferper. Pat asked the other two if he let them off in the meadow if they could climb up to the scene of the carnage and put the torn remains of the body into the basket. Once they had done that, he would winch it up and take it to the meadow and then pick them up.

They did as he asked, but when they got to the meadow, Joie told Pat to leave him there and come back for him later and bring a basket. Joie went back and skinned the big guy out and was waiting when the chopper returned. But by this time, the COs had gotten wind of what had happened and came out with Pat. They wanted to see how the accident happened, but Pat told them they should go out the next day because the light was fading fast and he did not want to be out there in the dark.

Joie loaded the hide into the basket and went down to meet them in the meadow. When he got into the chopper, the CO said, "Thank you, Joie, for skinning the bear out."

Joie gave him a hard stare and said, "If you skin him, he is yours. If I skin him, he is mine."

Pat gave Joie his pickup to go and get some salt so he could salt down the hide to keep the hair from slipping. Joie told Pat that the hunter had shot him four times. He said he'd had a hard time skinning that big guy because he was his friend.

Pat told him he understood, but now that it was all over, Joie could look after him and he would hurt no more.

The CO took a report from the hunter and charged him for being an accomplice to killing a bear out of season without a license. Then they got Pat to take them out to bring in the bear's body so they could do all their checking of ballistics to match it to the hunter's gun. They found his gun, and it had big bite marks on it. They had a hard time to just roll Ferper into the basket.

When they were done, they asked Joie if he wanted the body to bury it, and he told them to bring it out to his retreat and he would bury him there. He had a backhoe coming from the mine, and he dug a hole to put the body in. He made a cross and a headstone which read, "The Big Guy." Later when he got the grizzly mounted, he built a roof over the mount and had a plaque beside it that read, "My Friend, the Big Guy" along with a short story about his life.

This was right near the story pit. People came from all over the world to see the huge grizzle. It was a real tourist attraction and was advertised in a lot of places as a must see. Some of his measurements were the following: height, 10 feet 2 inches; weight, 1,175 pounds; hind foot, 14 inches long; front paw, width 9 and 3/4 inches; skull, 22 and 5/8 inches; and front claw, 6 and 7/8 inches long.

Joie was proud to tell stories of his big friend to all who wanted to listen about how he and the big guy sat outside his cabin and ate bannock together and how the bear saved his life. It kept his retreat full summer and winter. And the tourists really enjoyed it.

SECTION 3

Billy the Kid: A Mountain Goat

This goat lives in the high places and enjoys life from four to eight thousand feet above sea level. He is equipped with an exceptional good set of eyes and four exceptionally good feet. He truly is a mountain climber. He can be found in most of the Rocky Mountains.

In the Caribou Mountains and the Coast Range, he will come lower down to seek out mineral licks but prefers cooler and higher country. He is related to the antelope family. He wears a white hairy woolly coat and can stand exceptionally cold windy conditions.

His enemies are mainly man and eagles. But the ever-persisting predator the wolf has found a way to add the mountain goat to his list of prey. The wolf usually stays lower down in the mountains and hunts for his meals in the valleys where there is a lot more game. He prefers to live on deer but will take on elk, moose, caribou, or pretty much anything he can kill. They quite often come in to prey on domestic animals. When they run in larger packs, they are a real killing machine.

They will even drag a bear out of hibernation and kill it. Deep snow is somewhat of a problem to him as it makes his travel a lot harder. That is why he prefers to stay lower down in the more heavily timbered valleys. He likes the shelter of the timber when the winter storms blow. But as more and more snowmobilers seek the thrill of the alpines, it is providing him with a highway to the goat and caribou. And once he is up there, he will add them to his menu.

The caribou meat is considered very tasty to man, especially the younger animals. Eagles have been known to dive down on goat and knock them off the cliff and then go down and enjoy a tasty tenderized meal. The young can sometimes be snatched away from off the cliffs, but the mother is very protective of her young and keeps a close eye on any eagle that is flying around.

Tourists are attracted to them because of their white color, which makes them easy to be spotted in the parks. They do not like to be harassed by the industry and will move if they have the option.

There is a big difference between sheep and goats. Goats have a flatter body where sheep have a rounder muscle and are very fast on their feet. A goat will pick his way over and along steep places, but a sheep will run and jump from one rock to another and do it at a much greater speed. They are both very agile, and it is simply amazing where they can go and what they can do. In the summertime, they love the very high places, That is where they can sometimes get into danger as the ever-watchful eagle that is circling around looking for his next meal will swoop down and try to steal a young kid or try to knock an adult off-balance to cause him to go tumbling down to his death. The eagles will then fly down and enjoy a tenderized meal of goat.

Billy the Kid was introduced to his feathered friends early in life. It was early one morning while he was still getting used to his feet that an eagle decided he would make a good breakfast. The eagle swooped down to pick him off the ledge that he was sharing with his mother. She must have heard the swish of his wings, and in the last moment, she tipped her head and drove her sharp horns into him. But in doing so, she nearly knocked Billy off the ledge.

That was lesson number 1, and he would remember that noise of the eagle's wings it was filed in his memory bank, and it give him that little edge in time to get prepared for the attack that was coming.

It was a few years later that Billy was almost knocked off a ledge by two golden eagles that had taken an advantage of him. He was feeding on a very narrow ledge, and his taste for that nice, juicy grass overruled his better judgment of safety. As they swooped down to knock him off that ledge, they were not able to get a good hold of him, and each time they tried, they only got a claw full of hair. But there were two of them, and they nearly did succeed in getting him off his feet several times before he could recover before the next attack came. He had to back up to get to a place where he could turn around and get to safety.

Being a goat is like flying an airplane: mistakes are usually made high up, and it's the landing that usually kills you. That was lesson number 2: never put yourself in a position where you jeopardize safety. And always leave yourself an escape route.

Yes, he was a billy and someday would be king of the mountains a monarch in his own right. But first he had to learn all the rules by which this game was played. One slip and a fall could be fatal, or a slipup on how observant he was could cost him his life. Should a hunter find him too relaxed and careless, he could end up on some hunters' wall as a trophy of the high country.

He had gone down to a small stream to get his drink of water and was working his way back up to a pinnacle where he had lain down many times to chew his cud and keep a close eye on the surroundings below him. While he was working his way back over the broken rock from that little stream, he was spotted by two very observant hunters. Their rangefinder told them that they were 450 yards from him. Not an impossible shot, but a long one. They decided to try and get a little closer. As they were working their way down, one of them stepped on a loose rock, and it sloughed.

That was all it took for Billy to know he was in danger. As he moved from one big rock to another, he managed to get to the safety of some crags where he could hide. The day was on his side as daylight was quickly fading. As he stood there in complete silence in the darkness of that crag, the thought went through his mind that just maybe he had gotten to live to see another day.

The hunters camped out on top of that mountain and were sure they would get their goat tomorrow. But Billy was up early and in the dawn of morning made his move and was long gone by the time the hunters started their search for him. From very high up on a pinnacle, he watched the hunters spend most of the day looking for him. They were two very persistent goat hunters. As he lay there, he wondered if his body would end up in a pile of bleached bones on some faraway mountain or if the hunters would return to claim him for their trophy room. Only the shadow knows.

Mother Nature provides a school for each and every animal in her kingdom, but they must be willing to go to school to learn how to survive. Billy had gone to school and had learned quite well; that is why he had lived to become an old goat and had many a laugh at the hunter that sought his head. The moral of the story is if you want to live long enough to be a smart old goat, you have to go to school.

It was a nice, sunny day, and Billy was enjoying the warmth of the sun as he lay by the shelter of some juniper bushes. He was almost dozing off as the warmth of the sun felt so good, and it was making him sleepy. He had just finished filling up on some lichen and was chewing his cud and enjoying the wonderful scenery.

That was when he saw the wolves; there were six of them trotting along in single file. He did not know if he should just lay still and see if they would go right on by or get up and make a run for the rocky peak of that mountain. He did not know if he could outrun them, but as they started to spread out and sniff the mountainside, he became a little nervous.

They were much too close to him. He got up and started to walk up toward the rocky part of the mountain, but he had not gotten too far when they spotted him. Now the chase was on; he did his best to make it to the rocky part of that mountain, but they were closing in on him fast.

He made it to where the boulders had broken off the main part of the mountain that had been caused by frost and erosion. If he could make it into those big rocks, he just might beat them up the side of that mountain. But they were right on his heels, and while the broken-up rocks seemed to slow them down, they were much too close.

Billy was really puffing, but the race was not quite over yet. He was running so fast that he really did not have time to pick a good spot to make his stand. His intention was to go much higher, but he found himself boxed in and had barely enough room to turn around.

As he turned around, there was a big black wolf determined to reach out and grab him. Billy lowered his head and charged him. His horns dug into the wolf's neck and drove him off the rock that Billy was standing on. That knocked the wolf off to some rocks below, but the wolves just kept coming. He had gored several more, but they were wearing him down with exhaustion.

Then the wolves seemed to lose interest in him and started to run to where there was a steep drop-off. They had heard snow machines coming and were going to make a run for the safety of the drop-off. There were four men on machines. After they chased the wolves, they turned their machines around and came back to where Billy was.

He had waited too long to make his move to safety higher up on the mountain, but he needed time to just stand there for a few minutes and get his breath back. Now he did not know what was going to happen to him next. The men just sat there and took pictures of him. When he got his wind back, he came back out of the little hole that had saved his life and worked his way up that big old mountain. He stayed there for several days to make sure that everything was safe. Then hunger got the best of him, and he came back down to where he could find something to eat.

He moved off that mountain because he was not too sure of what the snow machines were all about, but he knew he did not like them. The wolves he had encounters with before and knew they were ruthless killers and would most likely be back. It was going to be risky because he would have to come down to the tree line and the snow could be deep, but he did not feel safe on this mountain.

He trudged through deep snow, and his diet for the next several days was fir and balsam tips; not the tastiest meal he had ever eaten. His persistence finally paid off when he got to a big old rocky mountain and the south slope had some good feed, and that helped pull him through the winter.

His experiences had made him an older and wiser goat. On this mountain, there were several nannies and kids. Even in his thin condition, he was looking forward to spring when the warmer winds would once more blow through the mountains.

The summer sun was such a welcome sight to the goats that they all shed out of their winter coats and had gained all their weight back. The little kids played ever so dangerously on the cliffs. But to a goat, it was just a normal day, and it was important to practice their mountain climbing skills, a skill that only a mountain goat has.

Billy made that his mountain his home. He liked the view that he got when he went a way up on the peaks of that mountain. It made him feel like he was a real king. Five years later, when he lay down to take that long, he knew he had left a lot of progeny to carry on the genes of a wise old goat.

SECTION 4

The Bighorn Sheep

In British Columbia, there are several different kinds of sheep: the bighorn, the California bighorn, the Stone, and the Dall. They are all prized for their size of horn.

The bighorn has a bigger base of horn and is probably considered the greatest prize of them all. And if you are a collector of heads, you will not be satisfied until you have the grand slam. The California bighorn is just a smaller version of the bighorn. They range in the more central and southern part of the province. The Stone is somewhat darker in color and have a wider curl to their horn. They range in the more northerly part of the province. The Dall probably has the widest curl of all to their horn and do the least brooming of the horn. *Brooming* is a term used to describe what sheep do to their horns when they become full curls so that they can see. They simply rub the tips off on the rocks of the mountains. They do this because they can't see past the end of the horn, and it interferes with their peripheral vision. Bighorns can broom as much as three inches off of their horns.

The Dalls are white in color and range in the more northerly regains of the province and into the Yukon and Alaska. The bighorn at one time ranged in great numbers in the foothills and the eastern part of the Rocky Mountains, but as time progressed, they learned that in order to survive, they had to move to the more remote regions of the Rocky Mountains.

The mountains are home to many different species of sheep. Mountains are built with a view to please the eye of every tourist, and they can glass the wild sheep from the different parks and resorts. At certain times you can find them right down town. Wild-sheep meat does not taste anything like mutton, and to every hunter, it is considered a delicacy.

When I am on a sheep hunt, if anyone in our camp is fortunate enough to get one, we usually don't bring any meat home; it gets all eaten up as camp meat. Sheep have exceptionally good eyesight. It is said that they can see as good as a man using an eight power set of glasses. The Indian described them as the animal that could see through rock. They have an instinct as where to look for their enemies. When they lie down to rest and chew their cud, they will position themselves so that they have all the angles covered, and it takes a good experienced hunter to sneak up on them.

One of the biggest mistakes hunters make is not using the glasses enough, and they need to stay off the ridges or the sheep will see you coming long before you see them.

Ewes, lambs, and the younger rams will ban together, but that does not mean that the more mature rams are not there. They just form bachelor clubs, and they are usually not that far away. In many cases, they can be spotted watching the herd from another mountaintop. I once spotted thirty-six lambs, ewes, and young rams in one bunch but could not find a mature ram amongst them. After moving to a different spotting location, I spotted five nice full curl rams across a valley on another mountain about two-thirds from the top. They were very well protected and had a bird's eye view of the herd.

In the rut, they will measure themselves for size, and if there is to be any disputes—and there usually are—they will settle them by bunting heads. They also strike their opponents with their front leg, and if they should be lucky enough to make contact with their opponent's scrotum, this will be sure to take the fight out of him.

This is a sight to see. They each back off a few steps and then charge at each other. Before their heads meet, they literally come off the ground and meet in midair head-on. Then they stand there looking a little bit stunned, only to do it all over again. The noise from that impact can be heard ringing across the valley. This can go on for a long while until one of them claims supremacy. But while this is going on, the younger rams get a taste of what love is all about. The banging of heads is an invitation to come and match your size and skills among all the sheep on the mountain.

I am not sure just what the rules are in this game, but eventually one ram will get to reign supreme over the rest, but he takes a real beating and don't often live to see the flowers bloom in the springtime. He can be so beaten up that the winter will decide his fate. Their noses get broken and sometimes take a long time to heal. The rams that get beaten out will often try to steal a few ewes and start a band of their own. But there seems to always be a few of the older ewes that will not breed with the younger rams, but when the old supreme ram approaches her, she will willingly stand for him. I don't know if that is Mother Nature's way of assuring that the supreme genes get to be carried on or not.

The sex drive is very strong during the rut, and sometimes when a ewe is in full estrus, she will get bred by three or four rams; not because she is always willing but because she is simply overpowered. Even if she lies down, a ram will paw on her until she gets up and then he will service her.

Sometimes that may be because she simply has no place to go to get away. The hand of man has not always been kind to the sheep. They have suffered devastating losses to the diseases that have been introduced by domesticated sheep and cattle sharing the same ranges of the foothills. When the pastures are grazed off, the sheep are left to find enough feed to sustain them for the winter while the cattle go back to the ranches where they are fed hay for the winter or graze on pastures that have been left just for winter grazing.

I have a friend who was a big-game guide, and he had a herd of fifty wild sheep in his territory that he looked after real well. In fact, so well that I think it is safe to say that his little herd of sheep was the only herd to be vaccinated against lung worms and parasites. He gave the sheep shots with A, D, and E and had the healthiest herd in the mountains. He knew the actual size of their horns and testicles because he had measured them.

It wasn't long before the Fish and Wildlife Officers were coming to him and asking him how come his little herd was doing so well. He told them, "You don't see any of my cattle sick, do you? That's because I look after them. If you look after the sheep in your area, they will look like that too."

They asked him if they could take a few and transplant them into another area. He could hardly say no, but he told them that they needed to clean up the other herd first. They asked him how they could do that, and he said, "Well, first, you have to know what you want to treat them for and then you have to treat them."

They said that would be imposable, so he said, "Well, you see, you know more than me, and we haven't got started yet, so I don't think I can help you." But they watched his little herd, and when the ewes were having twins, they wanted to come and get more sheep from his herd. That is when he said, "You should be giving me a larger quota not taking my sheep away from me."

It's kind of sad when a rancher can solve a problem for them and they can't figure it out for themselves. When the sheep came down off the mountain in the fall, he would have the choicest alfalfa out by the barn to feed them. Under a canopy of a net that was suspended by some poles, there was a long rope attached that ran to his house, and when the time was right, the net was dropped. And then veterinarian work was performed.

Rams are such majestic animals, and that is why they are sought after so much. They get auctioned off at clubs for thousands and thousands of dollars just for the right to hunt a world-class ram.

I feel so privileged to have lived in a country where we can enjoy the freedom to hunt and fish, and if we to have a deep-enough pocket, we can get a chance at a ram like that. And yes, times are changing and the good old days are gone, but it's not too late to roll up our sleeves and do our part to see that all is not lost forever.

I have felt so privileged to have been able to have sat in class of many different species and learned to understand their ways and language, even if it was just in a minute degree. And I still sign up for class every chance I get. It's been six years now that I have not gone out hunting to kill something. But I never miss the chance to take my camera and just get lost for a few hours or an afternoon just to see what I can learn. I believe the best teacher is learning it right from the source.

If you want to learn about a horse, learn it from the horse. And so it is with other species. Not to say others haven't been there and done that, but the hands-on approach is a must. Have you ever seen someone trying to lead a horse and they are pulling on one end of the rope and the horse is pulling on the other end? Who do you think is going to win? Animals learn to respond to the release of pressure, and we need to learn from that. They will tell you lots of things. All we have to do is learn it from them, and by that, I mean to learn their language. And once we have learned their language, things go a lot smoother.

The rams that I had been watching and following were getting used to me as long as I did not push them too much. If I would give them their space, I could stay within a hundred yards of them. I put out a flag, and their curiosity would get the best of them, and they would have to come and check it out.

I learned a lot from them that way. If a ram was lying down chewing his cud and if another ram with more seniority wanted to lie down, he would go and paw on the lesser ram until it got up, and then he would lie down in his bed. Whenever the rams were going for a drink of water or to a new feeding area, the boss ram was most always in the lead.

As the rut draws near, the rams do a lot more sparring with each other. They walk up to each other and show off their horns by tilting their heads first one way then the other way. They sometimes strike their front foot at each other. One can clearly see that there is a major change coming. They bunt heads a lot and get into some pretty serious scraps even before the rut really starts.

Then one day, a stranger came for a visit and was met by the boss ram. They did their show off horns, but then they were into the real rough stuff. I would have to say it must have taken a lot of nerve for him to come into a strange club because he got hammered by all the bigger rams. But he looked like an old boxer that had been in a few fights. His nose had been broken and one ear was split, but he showed no fear. And they even tried to gang up on him and bunt him from the side, and I thought they were for sure going to cripple him, but he took them all on. When the match was over, he stood the boss ram of all of them.

He then walked off that mountain to claim his prize and went to the band of ewes and lambs. He checked them out and seemed to be satisfied. The next day, the small band of rams that I had been camping with went to join the ewes, so I went along with them but stayed back a little farther so not to cause any problem for them. The new boss ram came out to meet them, and the fight was on again. He was one tough ram; not only could he dish out the punishment but he also could take it as well. He showed no mercy once when he was in battle with another more mature ram. A lesser ram came in from the side and was going to smash him in the ribs, but that boss ram did a lightning-quick turn and flattened him. Before he could recover, the boss ram gave him one on the front shoulder that may have broken it.

I stayed long enough to get better acquainted with some of the lambs, but the older ewes were the hardest to become friends with. My food was getting desperately low, so I decided to leave while the weather was still kind to me. I was hoping to spend the entire rut with them to see just how that boss ram made out. I do believe one could have gotten very well acquainted with those little lambs. It was funny to watch the old girls. When one of the lambs would get too close to me, they would stomp their front foot as much as if to tell the lambs "That's close enough."

When I returned to that herd the next summer, I didn't know if I was going to find the new boss ram or not. Was he going to be with the old bachelors club, or had they run him off? I found the lambs and ewes first, but they wanted no part of me. Then I spotted a nice big ram coming out of some shin tangle as I watched him for a little while. It appeared that there were more in there, so I just waited them out. Sure enough, there were six of them, but there should have been seven.

Did the younger ram with the injured shoulder succumb to the winter? But on closer inspection, the old broken nose was still there. They looked like old buddies that had never had a scrap in their life before. I set up my little tent right out in the open where they could see me at about five hundred yards. Then I set up my little flag and set back to see how they would react to it. It took most of the afternoon for them to come and check it out, and they never came closer than a hundred yards. I could tell they were spooked. That big boss ram did not trust me being there.

So I picked up a pot and walked back away from them to get some water so I could make tea. When I got back to where I could see the tent, they were all standing around inspecting it. I spoke real softly to them, but even that kind of talk spooked them. But they did not go very far. I just went about making my tea as if they were not even there. But when I turned the camp stove on, it spooked them again, but their curiosity soon got the best of them, and they slowly come sneaking back to investigate what was making that noise.

I talked to them just like they were my company, which they really were. Then I made me a cup of soup, and their curiosity or the smell of the soup drew them even closer. I should have been taking pictures but did not want to spook them. At times it was almost scary as they were all around me. When the soup was done, I shut the stove off, and their curiosity seemed to drop off. They began to feed but kept a sharp eye on me.

That summer they had an intruder. A wolverine came calling looking for a meal of lamb and just may have found one or two. But I helped to persuade him that it was to his best interest to go look for a marmot on some other mountain. It was when he decided that maybe he could find a free meal from me that I used my .38 Magnum as a persuader. It sure worked, but it took me a week to settle the sheep down again.

A wolverine can sure make a mess of a tent in short order, but I had no other choice. One night, I was awakened by him trying to get into my tent. And he was so persistent that I had to throw my shoe at him to get him to leave. Then he wanted to pack my shoe off. It was quite a sight to see me in the very early hours of the morning with barely enough light to see throwing stones at a wolverine that was trying to steal my shoe. That's when I said, "That's enough, bud."

As the summer began turning into fall, there was evidence of change that was coming, and soon, the rut would be on. The rams were flexing their muscles and feeling macho. Two of the bigger rams from the herd of ewes joined the bachelor club and accepted their rank and place in the club.

I left the mountain to restock my supplies so that I could be back for the rut. As I was leaving, I stopped to have one last look at the rams. They were all watching me leave, and they no doubt were wondering what I was going to do. I restocked my supplies and equipped myself with winter clothing for the weather that was to come.

Up to this point, my stay with the sheep was an amazing experience. But what was to come was something that I was not quite as well prepared for as I thought. The weather started out just beautiful, but when the winter winds blow off those snow peaks, let me tell you, it gets damn cold. And hanging your butt over a drop-off with the wind coming up at fifty miles an hour can freeze your family jewels as hard as the brass balls of a monkey. But like a war, the rut goes on, and to the sheep, it was just another day in the cycle of life.

But when I saw icicles hanging off the pubic hair on the sheep's sheath, I must admit I thought of warmer climes. When the storms would move in, the sheep would move lower down to the shelter of the trees at timberline. The thing was that they always knew a day ahead of me and would be well into the move before I even got started. The cold did not seem to bother them. They would just spar a little harder with each other, and the frost from their breath and heat of body would contribute to the making of new clouds.

Something that never stopped was the bunting of heads. I never did witness a knockout or a broken neck but did see some get quite severely injured when they were rammed from the side. For one to watch two mature rams meet head-on in midair, you will see the shifting of what looks like the whole body move two inches toward the front of the ram. The stop is so sudden one has a hard time to understand how the rest of the body can stand that, yet they will do that over and over again. Their horns seem to be unbreakable, yet I have seen rams with a broken horn, and they seem to be doing quite well, except they are a little out of balance.

Yet when the rut is over, it's over, and the time has come to rejoin the bachelor club once more. All is forgiven and forgotten. For animals that beat their heads together as much as they do, you would think that their brains would be so scrambled that they would not know up from down, but even in their older years, sheep are a very intelligent animal.

With a little help and cooperation from their two-legged predators, they should be around for a long time doing what they know best, and that is raising more sheep. But should man abuse their rights, the sheep too could go the way like other species, and that would be a very sad day.

As I sat there looking over that little bunch of sheep, I wondered just how much damage I had done to those sheep. They had learned to trust me, and I had gained a great deal of knowledge from them, but would someone come in to take their life just for the sake of having a head on his wall? I hoped not. I hoped that they would revert back to their wild instincts and be sheep as I first found them. And I am sure they will. Just maybe I'll get to go back and visit that little herd someday before these old legs quit pumping on me.

SECTION 5

Rudolph, the Caribou

The caribou is a very interesting animal, and one that has been around for many, many years. It is a herd animal and prefers to live in big bunches. It is somewhat smaller than an elk or a moose but is quite a bit bigger than a deer. The males and females both have horns, but the males grow huge horns, and on a mature bull, the top beam will have a palm with points that grow off that. The other thing that they have is a horn that grows off the main beam and down over the nose. This is called a shovel, and it assists them in breaking up the hard crusty snow. They have a rather large foot that enables them to walk on top of the snow much more easily. They are and can be browsers but prefer to graze on a plant called lichen that grows high up on the mountain or on the tundra. However, they will browse young birch and willow tips.

They are migratory animals and will travel hundreds of miles to get to their calving grounds. They are exceptionally good swimmers and think nothing of swimming across a lake that is five or six miles wide. They are somewhat shorter in leg than a moose or an elk, but when they are on the move, they can trot for hours. There are two types of caribou in Canada: the woodland and the barren-land. The wood land is the bigger of the two.

The caribou have been domesticated in some countries, and they are used to pull sleighs. That may very well be where Santa got the idea. Their meat is very tasty, except when they are in the rut. The bulls can be very strong. The mature bulls are somewhat majestic with their big horns and the creamy white color that runs midway from their front shoulders to nearly the ears.

Around their feet, they have that creamy white hair that is longer than anywhere else on their body.

Caribou are under a lot of pressure from more than one or two sources. The barren-land herds have always lived with the wolves and bears, and yes, this has taken a toll. There are wolf packs that simply follow the caribou and live off them. It is true that they kill the old, weak, and crippled ones, but they also are responsible for crippling a lot of them, only to kill them later as they become weak and can no longer keep up to the herd.

The natives depend on the caribou for their food and clothing as well, and so the pendulum of Mother Nature swings back and forth and keeps a balance. But the ever-expanding demand for oil, gas, and minerals no doubt has had an impact on them as well. It is when we, man, have decided to do things for our good that we change the balance of nature. It would be nice to see the resource users all come together and try to work out a solution that would be beneficial to all.

The barren-land herd runs in numbers of thousands, but the woodland caribou do not run in as large a herd, and therefore, the predators like wolf and bear can have a very devastating effect on them. But most of all, I believe that the females should be off-limits to all interaction with people when the herd numbers are declining.

Those herds that winter high up on the alpines are relatively safe from predators, but when the snow machines pack a trail up to where the caribou are, they are making a highway for the wolf to run on, and a herd of fifty caribou can be wiped out by a pack of eight or ten wolves. They will feed off that herd until they are starved or are worried to death.

I have hunted caribou, and now one hangs in my den on the wall. The meat was delicious, and I consider myself very privileged to have had the chance to get one. I am no longer interested in killing another one just for the bragging rights since then I have watched two big bulls battle for the right to be the boss and claim the herd. I had a front seat in Mother Nature's theater. The grunting and the clashing of horns will forever be embedded in my mind as I watched them battle, and I am grateful for the opportunity.

The native people use the hide for clothing. They tan the hide with the hair on, and it is an exceptionally good windbreaker. They use it for mitts and moccasins as well. To see a herd of ten or fifteen caribou on a mountainside right from my camp is more rewarding to me than having to pack one out and a lot less work.

To me, a successful hunt is when one can go out and see animals and study them and their ways. That is why I like to hunt with horses. I like to get way back into the mountains where no one will bother me or disturb the animals that I find.

One thing that I found is that horses don't seem to like the smell of a caribou. One day, my hunting partner and I went hunting for a couple of goats. We had a rather tough climb, and after we got our goats back to the horses, daylight was fast eluding us, but I knew the horses would know their way back to camp. Rather than sleeping out under a spruce tree, I decided we could make it back to camp.

We were doing real well, and we had made it off the steepest part of the mountain by about 9:00 PM. There was about a half moon shinning, and being that we were now in the meadow, I was relaxed and was just enjoying myself. It had been a hard climb, and I was tired and a bit on the sleepy side. I kept dozing off when all of a sudden, my horse let out one hell of snort, and it was amazing how fast I came alive. It is a good thing he didn't jump sideways, or I just may have ended up on the ground. Instead, he just seemed to drop a foot under me.

The first thing I thought was we had run into a grizzly. He snorted a couple more times, and I saw the white rumps of caribou go bounding off into the darkness. It was a good thing it wasn't a grizzly because he would have had me. I didn't even get my gun out of the scabbard. I dropped the goat cape that was draped across the saddle, and I was a clawing for leather. My partner called out, asking, "What the hell is going on up there?"

I said, "Oh, I just dropped my goat."

He was all for sleeping out under a spruce tree because he thought it was too dangerous to be packing fresh meat that late at night, and he probably was right. When we made it to the cabin, I wanted to bring the meat and hides inside because we didn't have a hanging tree made yet, but that is where he drew a line in the sand.

He said, "If you are going to do that, I am going to go sleep in the shitter, and you can wrestle with the grizzly."

He was not just a hunting partner—he was a very good hunting partner. He had a lot of experience when it came to hunting, and I knew he was probably right. In the morning, the first thing that I did was check to see if the goats were still there, and they were.

I said to Leo, my hunting partner, "See? The grizzly didn't come and steal the goats."

He said, "Do you know why? I tell you, Lloyd. The way you were snoring, not even a grizzly would come near this cabin."

One has too always be thinking outside the box, and so often, we forget to consider all the facts that will keep us safe while we wander through Mother Nature's wilderness. Leo, my hunting partner, was a few years older than me and had made a few mistakes in his many trips into the mountains. But he learned from them very well, and that is why it was so good to go with him. Now he has gone up yonder and is probably sitting by the campfire drinking his cowboy coffee, waiting for me and wondering what is taking me so long. Can you imagine the long conversation we will have? It could go on and on and on forever.

I do not know if our paths will ever cross again, but if they do, whether we will be shoveling coal or polishing the pearly gates, I can hear him saying in his jovial way, "You know, Lloyd, only a Frenchman or a Polack could do a job like this." It is very interesting how at one time in our lives we may not have had very much in common, but as the saying goes, when the time is right, the teacher will appear. The time was right for Leo to have spent his last years here on this earth with me. We enjoyed each other so much and shared so many things together. I am not sure who the message was, for him or me, but the timing was right.

Was he meant to be the last teacher in my life in order for me to graduate in the knowledge of animals that live in the wilderness of the Great Creator? My father and Indian friends were very important in shaping my life in the ways of hunting, but it seemed to be Leo who could sit down with me. We could talk for hours about animals and their habits and way of life. And that is what made the time we spent out in the mountains so enjoyable. As you read through this book, you will read of the knowledge one can only get from learning it from the animals that live in this wonderful creation.

I speak from the animal's point of how the animal felt or what they saw and thought. In this, I am using their imagination to the best of my ability as I have learned to understand them. When I first ventured into this way of life of hunting and gathering, my way of thinking was a lot different than now. Then it was necessary to hunt to put meat on the table, but as time went on, I learned to understand and appreciate the animals, and if I didn't need to harvest one, I didn't.

But the call of the mountains never stopped calling, and to spend time in them gave me a great scene of satisfaction to just be out there to listen, smell, and look upon such a wonderful creation. It can be kind or cruel; it all depends on our attitude and how we look at it. Few people see it the same and understand it the same way. I can say that I am very thankful that my paths led me where they did. I would not have wanted to miss or change any of it.

To understand is said to be the foundation of wisdom, and there is so much to understand that Mother Nature can teach us right from the smallest insect to great grizzly bear. And if we plan to venture out into the wilderness, it is advisable to learn as much as we can about it. The tiny ant can and will put the run on much-bigger animals if one should enter into its space. The mouse can put the lady of the house up on the couch or the table. The grizzly will often fight to its death should you inter into its private cache, but to understand each of these critters will safely lead you through the wilderness, and you should come away with a better understanding. A good rule of thumb is to always leave an escape route for them to leave, and they will usually take it.

I have used many an old cabin that has been abandoned, and with a little persuasion, the porcupines, squirrels, and mice leave, and with a little spit and polish, the place is quite livable. The mice and squirrels will quite often come back as soon as all is quiet. They want to see what you have left for them to feast on.

One thing we have learned that from the smallest to the largest, they will all fight to protect their right. The ant will bite you, the bee will sting you, and the grizzly will kill you if he has to. To understand these animals in the wild can and will make your time in the wilderness a pleasant experience. One should not get discouraged, and one should expect to learn it in one outing or all at one time. After all, one does not learn to work the stock market or the computer or fly the passenger jet in one outing. However, when you do learn, it is very rewarding, and you will enjoy that part of the world that so many people miss.

Section 6

Incidents in My Lifetime of Hunting and Being with Animals of the Wild

For those of you who enjoy the hunting aspect of this book, I will leave you with some of my most outstanding and hair-raising stories that I have had over the many years that I have been involved in hunting.

The first one is not so outstanding or hair-raising but came early in my life. It came before I was old enough to pack a gun. And the reason that is it happened that way was probably that my father knew if he let me pack a gun, he could not be with me everywhere I went, and some of the things that I would get myself into may have gotten me into more trouble than I could get myself out of.

This day, I was walking down to the lake to catch some fish to feed a few mink that I had caught in some of my live trap boxes. I had packed a slingshot in my hip pocket from when I was four years old, and I was good at it. This day, I was loaded for bear. There were always rabbits along the path to the lake, so I had my best bullet loaded in my slingshot: a steel ball bearing that I got from a bearing that had overheated on the planner mill and was discarded. That bearing gave me ten evenly matched bullets for my slingshot.

As I was walking ever so slowly along the path, looking for a rabbit, a deer stepped out onto the path not fifty feet in front of me. I think he was a bit surprised to see me. As he looked at me, I shot him right between the eyes. He went down, and I thought I had killed my first deer. But before I got to him, he jumped up and ran down the path to the lake. I ran down after him as he ran out into the lake, then he just stood there and looked at me. I bounced one more off his horn as I had shot a little bit high, and that made him go out into the lake. As he swam out, I ran back to get a gun from a native Indian who lived in an old log cabin. I guess he thought he better come and do the shooting.

When we got back to the lake, the deer was almost onshore. The Indian started shooting, and after he had shot him in the gut three or four times, he finally knocked the deer down. I asked him for the horns, but he would not give them to me. I told him how I had knocked him down with the slingshot but he didn't believe me. But when he skinned him out, I guess he decided to look and see if the deer was shot in the head, and he found where the bearing had hit the deer in the head. He said that if the shot was two inches higher, it may very well have killed the deer. I was thirteen years old, and what I lacked in size and age, I made up for in determination.

The next thing I did was when I was fourteen years old. I was home alone in the spring of the year in the logging camp that was near the Lesser Slave Lake in northern Alberta. The geese, ducks, swans, pelicans, and sandhill cranes were all in their migration to the north. They would fly over nonstop day and night. They were bucking a fairly strong head wind and, as a result, would fly lower.

So I got out the 30-06; I had lots of shells, but I had never shot that big of a gun before. As I lined up on these sandhillers, they looked like pretty big birds, so I touched one off. I had been concentrating on those birds that I did not see the guy coming across the yard to see if he could buy some cigarettes from the store that we had. That 30-06 kicked my shoulder so hard, that momentarily I forgot all about the birds. That guy said, "You got it, you got it!"

Sure enough, it come down in a sort of spiral and landed in the mill yard. We ran over to where it hit the ground, and it was still alive. I had just broken its wing. That was one of the biggest flukes I think I ever made.

That fall, my dad bought me a single-shot twelve-gauge Cooey shotgun and took me out shooting geese with him. We had a lot of fun. We slept beside a small lake where we made a bed out of willows that we lay down on top of bulrushes to keep us off the wet ground. Then we covered that with lots of bulrushes, and we lay down our sleeping bags on top of them. To finish things off, we covered that with more bulrushes so when the geese came in off the fields, we were ready for them.

We got six that night, but the most of them came after dark. My dad didn't want to shoot them because we could not see where they would fall in the bulrushes. But I could not contain myself and shot a few more. I could see them when we were looking into the sky, and they were so low you couldn't miss, but when they hit the ground, it was hard to find them.

During the night, they would fly so low over us we could hear the swishing of their wings. I don't think I slept a wink that night. You could hear them splash into the water when they landed, and it did not seem too far from our bed. Many of them seemed to be overfull and just groaned until the wee hours of the morning.

The ones that we picked up were so full of barley that it was coming out of their mouth. As soon as the first sign of daylight appeared, they started really making a lot of noise, and you could hear them flapping their wings, getting ready to head back to the fields. We got one more good shot in, and then they were all gone. I don't know just how many geese there were in that end of the marshy lake, but there must have been a thousand.

The other thing that kept me awake was that under my bed was four inches of water, and the only thing that kept me from sinking into the water was those willows and bulrushes. But my dad knew what he was doing when he made those beds, and all was well and dry in the morning.

In the morning, we picked up fourteen geese, and there were a few we could not get to. That was my initiation to bird hunting, and I had many a good hunts with my dad after that.

As I grew older, I bought a new pump shotgun from a good friend of mine, and because he knew a lot of the farmers in the area, he set up a hunt for a Sunday. It was to be more of a go-look-and-see than an actual hunt. We loaded up my dad's old Power Wagon and headed for some of the more remote stump farmers.

The roads were not very good, but the old Dodge could go mostly anywhere. You would not dare to go there without a four-wheel drive. We came to this gully. And Mike said, "Lloyd, let's leave the truck here, and we will walk to the other side of the gully."

We did that, but as we were coming up to the top of the gully, we heard some geese honking. Being I was a lot younger, I hurried up to the top, and there came nine geese. They were flying real low across the field.

If they kept coming the way they were flying, they should fly right between Mike and me. I told him to get ready, and when all the banging stopped, there was just dead silence. Mike said, "Lloyd, that is a dirty crying shame. We never left any for seed."

We picked up our geese and walked back to the truck. When we got there, Mike said, "You know, Lloyd, you are bad company. I sold you a good gun and you have only had it a week, and you don't have a plug in it anymore. I know now why we shot all those geese."

I said, "You bet. If you are going to keep score, you better take that plug out of your gun."

He said, "If Mary knew I was hunting with someone like you, she would never let me go."

Mike owned the hardware store in town and knew most of the farmers in the country. He would tell me where to go and see if any of the farmers were having a goose problem.

I was getting to the age where the girls were really nice company, and I would take them out hunting with me. So when I would go out scouting for places to hunt, I would load up the old Power Wagon with as many girls as I could find.

It was a real blast, and they practically stood in line just to come along. Well, Mike told me where I should go and see a few farmers because they had been in his store and were complaining that the geese were bothering their grain fields. I loaded five or six girls and went for a look-see.

Well, I found lots of geese, but when I went to the farmers' place to get permission, they were not too sure they wanted someone driving around on their fields. So I went back and told Mike that I had found lots of geese but that the farmers were not too sure they wanted me to hunt them. He called the farmers and asked them why they did not want him and me to hunt the geese. They told him that I had been there with a truck load of girls and they were not too sure that I was safe to be turned loose on their fields.

Mike hung up the phone and asked me to come into the store where he could talk to me without Mary hearing what he had to say. He said, "Lloyd, Lloyd . . . if I am going to hunt geese with you, the girls are going to have to go. Your hormones are on a different level than mine, and first of all, I could never handle those young girls at my age [he was in his early fifties]. And Mary would never let me forget that."

Every time Mike would come with me, I had to promise Mary that I would not be taking any girls along. They were really true friends, and I enjoyed them a lot.

One day Mike had a hunt all lined up for his friend and me. It was to be a morning hunt. They had the pits all dug and the decoys were set up, so all we had to do was to hunker down and wait for the geese to come. Well, they came but were not interested in our field.

We were standing up in our pits talking to each other when I hear this goose honk. I looked around, and here comes one lonely goose quite high. I ejected all my bird shot out and put in an SSG. I led that goose by a good foot and let one fly, and that goose came down deader than a nit. One pellet hit it in the head and killed it dead.

Mike turned to his friend and said, "That's my hunting partner."

The guy asked what the hell kind of a gun I shot anyway. Mike asked me later how the hell I pulled that one off, and I just told him that it was because of the good gun he sold me.

I guess it is only natural that I have had so many close encounters with moose as I have shot many of them, but some of them I did not shoot. One was when I came home from logging, and there was a cow moose and her two calves standing in my yard. As soon as I tried to get out of my pickup, that old girl took a run at me. She was one mad mama. When I thought I could make it, I ran to the house for all I could go, and she was right in my hip pocket by the time I got there. As I tried to open the door, I realized my wife had gone to town and locked the door. As I looked over my shoulder, the moose was standing four feet from me. Her ears were flat against her head, and those eyes looked like Oreo cookies; she was so close I could smell her breath (it smelled like fermented twigs). I just stood there and never made a move. Finally she turned around and went back to her calves.

It was in the fall of the year at Black Creek Ranch, and I was still making hay in some of the lowland that had flooded earlier. Jim, my hired man, was helping me do some repair work on the hay bine.

I said, "I think I have had enough of this monkey wrenching. Why don't we go moose hunting?"

He looked at me as if I had slipped a cog in my wheel and said, "What about this?"

I said, "If you want to shoot a moose, one is just walking across the field to the river."

In that case, he agreed we should go. I told him that I would drive, and when I slowed down, he was to step out and get ready to shoot the moose and I would just keep on driving. The moose would most likely stand and watch me drive away. All went as planned, except he shot him in the front leg. He shot again, and the moose went down. As we ran over to him, I could see he was not dead, so I told Jim to shoot him in the head. He did, but his shot was way too low, so I ran around and grabbed the moose by the horns, telling Jim to hurry up and cut his throat. But that moose must have under stood me and was getting up to leave the country, and I can't say I blame him. Jim, being the good cowboy that he was, grabbed him by the horns, and we wrestled him back onto his side. The moose was doing an awful lot of kicking with that hind leg, and I did not know how long I was going to keep him on his side but was scared to let him go.

Jim got the job done, and as we stood there looking at our moose, Jim said, "Is that the way you always kill them buggers?"

I said, "No, first I kill them when I shoot them. What is the matter with your gun?"

He said he didn't know, but it was not shooting where he'd aimed it. He said now that he knew I was that good at steer dogging, he was going to have to take me to town with him when he did his roping and steer dogging.

I was out hunting elk, and it was quit warm out. The elk were still up high on the mountains. We were not having much luck. So I decided to climb this mountain to see if there were any elk up there. The little trail I was trying to follow was really steep, and I had my gun strapped across my back and was not going too fast. In fact, I was doing a lot of resting, but I was nearly at the top as I stopped to have one more rest before I made it to the top. Unbeknownst to me, a mountain lion was sitting on a big rock above me, and as I looked up, he was in full flight coming at me. I could see those big paws and claws stretched out to get me.

Well, I let the most bloodcurdling yell out of me and hunkered as close to the path as I could. He landed six feet from me and made one more jump and was gone into the bush. He no doubt heard me coming but may have mistaken me for a sheep.

Sometimes you look for excitement, and other times it looks for you. I was doing the first shift of graveyard and was working for Fording Coal as a shift boss and was in the big dragline discussing with my operator the plan as to what it was that we were to do with the big machine. A radio call came in for me, and it was Romeo, the shifter from up on the mountain. He was at the carpenter shop picking up some standards to put the power cable on so the big haul trucks did not run over it.

He asked me to hurry up and come to the carpenter shop. He was the kind of guy who would play tricks on you if he could, like get you there and then ask you to help him load the standards. So I was in no hurry, but he called again in a minute or two and asked me where I was. I told him I was still at the dragline, and he told me to hurry up and get down there, so I said I would be right on my way.

As I was leaving the dragline, my operator said, "Sucker."

When I got there, Romeo said, "Do you see him? Look by the empty barrels."

There was a black bear looking over the top of the barrels.

Romeo told me that there were a couple of shop doors that were open and wondered if we could put him into the shop. I told him to let me get into the right position and then to the giver. When he bumped those barrels, that bear came out of there just a-flying. I hazed him into the back of the shop, and the first door that I came to, I steered him right in. He was really moving.

As I skidded my truck to a stop, Romeo was right there, asking where the bear went. I told him it had gone right into the shop. The bear ran under a big haul truck where two mechanics were working on the wheel motor and knocked over their Snap-On toolbox. Can you imagine what they were thinking? I will bet they thought they were hallucinating after coming off a long change where they had been partying across the US border at Kalispell.

About then, the bear had made his first trip around the shop and was looking for the open door. We were standing right there and threw our hard hats at him. That is when he started his second round. By now, most of the guys were in the machines and hiding wherever they could. Well, he saw the big window at the dispatch office and must have taken it for a hole in the wall. He made for it as hard as he could go. The dispatch guy was laughing at everyone else until the bear decided to jump through the window and did a spread eagle right in front of him and fell over backward. We damn near had to give that guy a first-aid treatment.

By this time too many people were getting involved, so we let the bear out of the shop. The security guard was looking for brownie points and called the mine superintendent and told him that somehow a bear had got into the shop and that Romeo and I might have had something to do with it.

In the morning, we were called into the personnel office and asked what we knew about a bear been in the shop. I said apparently there was one in there, and he created quite a bit of excitement. They then asked Romeo what part he had played in it. He suggested that before they went about trying to blame it on someone, maybe the doors should be kept closed on the shop at night. Nothing more was said, but Romeo and I got a hold of that little wimpy dispatcher and told him before he tried that again he better have his facts straight or we would fit him with a set of cement over shoes and throw him in the settling pond.

We were at home one night, and the evening was nice and warm and the door was open with only the screen door closed. I had finished my supper, and my wife had made spare ribs, and they were sure good. I was feeling a bit overfed and was relaxing in my reclining chair, watching TV, when the little border collie went tearing off the porch and was sure there was something around that shouldn't be there.

I went to have a look but couldn't see anything. I left the porch light on and went back to my chair. About half an hour later, there was another commotion, and this time I saw what the dog was after. It was a brown bear, about three hundred pounds. So I got my 25-06 and left the door open so I would not make a hole in my screen door.

When he came back again, he was right on my bottom step and I shot him. He was as fat as could be, and why he insisted he should come into the house, I will never know, and it doesn't matter. What matters is he will never bother anyone again.

I was out in the woodlot doing a bit of logging, and the day was going good. It was three in the afternoon, and I had a load all ready to go to town. I decided to skid a few more turns before I would quit for the day. I went out to get another turn of logs, and as I was putting the choker around the tree, I looked back, and there was a cougar standing on the same tree that I was putting the choker around. The cougar was very intent on me. The noise of the skidder did not scare him; he just looked at me. I yelled at him, and he just walked off the tree and stood there and watched me.

That can sure raise the hackles on the back of your neck. There were lots of deer for him to eat, and he looked in real good shape. If I had a gun, I sure would have shot him.

At times, wild animals can sure be very unpredictable. And when they lose that fear of man, they are also very dangerous. Just last year a grizzly walked through our neighborhood, through town, and has never been seen since. Possibly he was a displaced bear that was looking for a new territory, but we were glad he did not decide to stay in our area.

One of my early teachers in the art of hunting was an Indian who lived in northern Saskatchewan, and he hunted because that was how his family survived. Fish, rabbits, grouse, moose, deer, bears, and berries were what made up most of their diet. He hunted and shared it with the whole village when he needed too. My dad learned to speak his language, and in turn, he learned to speak English. Their Indian reserve bordered my dad's farm, and they were good neighbors. Charlie was out hunting like so many other times in his life, but this day, he nearly lost his life doing it. He hooked up his horses to the wagon, loaded up a few supplies, and drove his horses down an old wagon trail to where he hoped to kill several moose, and maybe some deer.

There were some other natives that were going to camp not too far from him, and they planned to get together later on in the hunt. Charlie found himself a good campsite by a little creek, but what he liked more was he had found a fresh moose track. So he tied his horses to a tree and went to hunt the moose before he set up his tent. He did not go too far when he spotted the moose, but he wanted to get a little closer. As he was sneaking up on the moose, he heard a branch break and looked to see what had broken the branch. To his surprise, it was a bear, and it was tracking him.

He tried to scare it off, but it was dead-set on him, so he shot it. The bear fell down but got up and kept coming at him. He shot it twice more, but it kept coming, so he waited until the bear was just a few feet from him. Charlie planned to shoot it in the head, but when he pulled the trigger, there was just a click; his gun was empty.

What happened in those next few minutes was very dramatic. The bear grabbed Charlie by the leg and flipped him on his back then tried to crawl on top of him, biting him on the legs and side. He tried to bite Charlie on the face, but Charlie grabbed the bear by the bottom jaw and wrestled with him and managed to roll him off. Before he could get to his feet, the bear was trying to bite his legs again. He kicked him off, but the bear had bitten right through his feet as he was only wearing moccasins. Then the bear managed to crawl on top of Charlie and ripped a hole in his side.

Later, Charlie said he was getting tired and could not see very well because so much blood was coming from the bear and getting on his face. He managed to grab the bear by the side of the head and he said he held him so he could not bite him. He said he could feel the bear start to get weaker and managed to roll him off. The bear died right there beside Charlie.

The reason Charlie's gun was empty was because he had lent it to a friend who had shot a deer with it using several shells and had not replaced them. Not too many men can say have they wrestled a bear to its death and lived to talk about it.

When he got up, he said in his Indian language, "Woah, woah. Lots of blood, like when you shoot 'em moose." Charlie was beaten up quite badly. The bear had bitten through his hands and feet and had bitten his legs above and below his knees. He was scratched quite badly as well. But the worst damage he suffered was where the bear ripped a hole in his side. He was bleeding from the many places that the bear had ripped, bitten, and scratched him, but when he got up, he said that his stomach wanted to fall out, so he put it back in the best he could and walked back to his horses.

He drove to where his buddies were to make their camp, and lucky for Charlie, they were just setting up the tent. By this time Charlie had passed out and was just lying in the wagon box. His buddies wrapped him in a blanket and drove him back to the reserve, which was somewhere between eight or ten miles. Then two Indians came to our place and wanted to borrow some iodine. My mom asked them what they needed the iodine for, and they said in their very broken English, "Bear scratch 'em Charlie."

So she went to tell my dad, who was working in the field, and he went to have a look at Charlie. Dad said Charlie was lying on a blanket and just moaning, and the Indians were all sitting around his bed singing and chanting. When Dad took a look at Charlie's wounds, he thought that Charlie was soon going to die. He said there were leaves, twigs, and dirt right in with his intestines. He bandaged him up the best he could with some clean flower sacks and took him to the trading post, and from there, they took him with a speeder on the railway tracks to a small town. From there, they called the Forest Ranger to come and take him by truck to the hospital.

And yes, he was still alive. He spent a few months in the hospital but fully recovered. It is a miracle that he never died with an infection as they did not have the antibiotics that we have now. I can still remember Charlie coming up the road to our house with his walking stick; he wanted to thank my dad for helping save his life. He showed us where the bear had bitten through his hands and feet and the ugly scar on his stomach.

There is no doubt that he was one tough Indian. It was not too long before he was out hunting moose again with his two sons. They seemed to take it all in stride, and life just continued on as if nothing had ever happened. They never dwelled on how badly they were hurt; the most important thing was that they had to hunt if they were to survive. Charlie lived to the ripe old age of ninety. The last time I saw him was in 1970, and he asked me to give his best regards to my mother and dad as we were living in Alberta then.

Some of these stories my seem to be a bit hard to believe, but I can assure you they did happen in my lifetime and have been such a learning experience, and now they have helped to make this book. I hope you have enjoyed them. Many happy trails, and watch for my next book, *A Chip Off the Old Block*, coming soon.

About the Author

Lloyd not only loves hunting and being in the outdoors but is truly in love with it. What makes his novels so compelling is that he has such a great understanding of the animals and the country in which they live. He has learned to understand them in a way not many have, to understand them and respect them for the strength they have, and to not try and make a human being of them.

Edwards Brothers Malloy
Thorofare, NJ USA
November 14, 2014